Princesses
Animals in Danger!

The girls stood in a circle with their hands joined in the middle.

"We promise to help all animals in trouble," said Emily.

The four rings glowed for a moment and Emily's heart missed a beat. Their adventures had only just begun!

Have you read?

The Wishing Pearl

💜

The Snow Jewel

💜

The Magic Rings

Look out for:

The Lost Gold

💜

The Shimmering Stone

💜

The Silver Locket

💜

The Ice Diamond

The Rescue Princesses
Animals in Danger!

Paula Harrison

nosy crow

THE SECRET PROMISE
THE MOONLIT MYSTERY
THE STOLEN CRYSTALS
All first published in the UK by Nosy Crow Ltd
All text © Paula Harrison, 2012
All cover illustrations © Sharon Tancredi, 2012
All interior illustrations © Artful Doodlers, 2012

This collection, ANIMALS IN DANGER, first published in the UK in 2013 by
Nosy Crow Ltd
The Crow's Nest, 10a Lant Street
London, SE1 1QR, UK

Text in this edition © Paula Harrison, 2013
Cover illustration in this edition © Sharon Tancredi, 2013
Interior illustrations in this edition © Artful Doodlers, 2013

Nosy Crow and associated logos are trademarks and/or registered
trademarks of Nosy Crow Ltd

Printed and bound in the UK by Clays Ltd, St Ives Plc
Papers used by Nosy Crow are made from wood grown in
sustainable forests.

ISBN: 978 0 85763 271 5

www.nosycrow.com

Contents

The Rescue Princesses
The Secret Promise

Paula Harrison

nosy crow

For Abby and Megan, true Princesses,
with all my love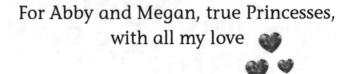

Chapter One

The Castle of Mistberg Forest

Princess Emily leaned right out of the carriage window, trying to get her first glimpse of the famous castle of Mistberg forest.

She'd waited nine years for her chance to visit and she couldn't wait a second longer. The forest air swept over her, sending her crown slipping sideways and her red curls flapping.

"Emily! Please don't push your head out of the window in that manner. It doesn't look very graceful," said her mum, straightening her own crown.

Princess Emily took one last look, then reluctantly drew her head back in. "You should have let me drive. I could have gone much faster than this."

Her dad's mouth twitched into a smile.

"The aim is to arrive in royal style," said her mum. "Not to shoot along like a racing car."

Emily resisted saying that racing would be more fun. Her mum and dad were the King and Queen of Middingland and they always knew the correct way to do things.

They had flown across the sea from Middingland that morning in the royal jet. Then they had ridden from the airfield in a carriage, because everyone arrived at the Mistberg Grand Ball by horse and carriage. The Ball took place

at King Gudland's castle every spring and was one of the biggest events of the season.

The scent of pine trees filled the carriage and Emily caught a flash of movement as a deer ran deeper into the forest. The horses pulling the carriage slowed down to a walk as they passed between a pair of gigantic golden gates.

The call of a peacock echoed across the grass. Emily held her breath. They must be inside the grounds of the castle! She stuck her head out of the window again, her heart drumming with excitement.

"Now, when we get inside we have a dress fitting at two o'clock," said the queen. "And you will remember to brush your hair, won't you? It's gone a bit wild in the breeze."

But Emily wasn't thinking about brushing her hair. Above her towered the

round turrets of King Gudland's castle,
stretching up to the sky.

Usually her little sister would have
nudged her out of the way, but Lottie was
staying with their cousins to recover from
a bout of chickenpox, so for once, Emily
had a perfect view.

The castle was much more magnificent
than their palace in Middingland and
she had three whole days to explore it.

A short, white-haired man hurried
down the flight of steps as the carriage
drew to a halt.

"Philip! Maria! How lovely to see you!"
he exclaimed.

"Hermann, how are you?" said Emily's
mum, stepping gracefully down from the
carriage. She turned to her daughter.
"Emily, I'd like you to meet King
Gudland."

"A pleasure to meet you, Princess," said

King Gudland.

Emily made a curtsy. She instantly liked the small man with his twinkly eyes. She hoped all the other kings and queens were as friendly as he was.

The purpose of the Mistberg Grand Ball was for young princes and princesses, aged nine or older, to present themselves to the twenty royal families from around the world.

Emily had never been before because her parents had been so busy with their royal duties at home in the kingdom of Middingland. But this year was different; Emily was now old enough to take part in the ceremony.

In three days' time she would have to curtsy in front of each and every king and queen, and she was already a little nervous.

"Come this way, Your Majesties," said

King Gudland, and he led them through an enormous hallway full of people hurrying around with suitcases.

They climbed up five spiralling staircases watched by the solemn pictures of King Gudland's ancestors. When they reached the top the king waved his hand towards three wooden doors.

"This is the West Tower, with my very comfiest rooms," he said. "The banquet begins at six o'clock. Don't be late!" And he gave Emily another twinkly smile before stepping back down the staircase.

"That's your room, Emily," said her mum, pointing to the first door. "Meet me in the dressmaking suite in half an hour. It's two staircases down and then turn right. You can't miss it."

Emily nodded, pushed her door open and took her first look at her room. A four-poster bed filled one corner and a soft, velvety sofa sat in the other. But Emily was drawn to the window, and when she got closer she realised that she was very near the top of the tower.

Everything on the ground looked tiny. She could see the stables for King Gudland's horses and a set of obstacles that looked like a huge adventure playground.

As she stared down, another carriage drew up in front of the castle and a girl dressed in green climbed out.

Emily watched her eagerly. She was looking forward to meeting some more princesses of her own age. Life at home in her palace in Middingland was great, but there was only her little sister to play with.

Suddenly Emily looked at her watch. Half an hour had flown by while she was daydreaming at the window. She was supposed to be in the dressmaking suite with her mum right now!

She rushed straight out of her room and back to the staircase. What had her mum said? Two staircases down? Yes, that was it.

She raced down the two sets of spiralling steps so fast that she began to feel dizzy. At the bottom she stopped, looking left then right. Which one was it?

Emily turned left. There was only one door in the passageway. That must have been why Mum had said she wouldn't miss it.

As she opened the door, she heard a man's deep voice. It sounded as cold as glass.

"There must be absolute secrecy, you understand? I will not put up with ridiculous mistakes," said the voice.

"Yes, My Lord. We understand," came

the reply.

Emily stopped uncertainly. The man with the deep voice had his back to her. He was clearly very rich, wearing a dark cape and a purple hat trimmed with furry material. The other two men nodded their heads humbly, their eyes fixed on the rich man.

This wasn't the dressmaking suite. She must have turned the wrong way. Emily started to tiptoe backwards. But the man with the deep voice swung round.

"What do you think you're doing? Come back, right now!" he barked, striding towards her.

Emily knew she had no explanations good enough for a man who barked like that. Spinning round, she ran back to the stairwell, her feet thudding across the red carpet.

She rushed down the opposite corridor,

tearing open the first door and landing inside the dressmaking suite in a tangle of arms and legs.

Chapter Two

The Other Princesses

"Emily!" Her mum's face froze into a frown. "Why on earth are you charging around like this?"

"I went the wrong way," gasped Emily. "And when I opened the door there was a—" She stopped, suddenly aware of all the eyes that were fixed on her.

Three other princesses stood nearby with their mums, while dressmakers fussed around them with pins and tape measures.

Emily picked herself up, feeling shy.

"Well, never mind," said Queen Maria with a sigh. "Now that you're finally here, please come and try this dress on. We must have it fitting properly for the Grand Ball on Saturday."

Emily followed her into the middle of the room. There were mirrors everywhere and long shelves that stretched all the way along one wall.

The highest shelf was covered with necklaces made of gold and silver. The middle one was full of shiny satin gloves and the lowest shelf had rows of party shoes covered in glittering stones.

Emily looked longingly at the necklaces. She'd brought her own ruby necklace in her suitcase but she knew her mum would make her save it until the night of the Grand Ball.

She went into a cubicle and pulled

the dress over her head. It was a pink ball gown made of smooth satin and decorated with red flowers.

When she came out and looked in a mirror, her heart leapt. This dress was the most beautiful one she'd ever had. Her long red hair curled over the satin material and her hazel eyes shone brightly.

"Stand up really straight, please, Emily," said her mum, fastening the buttons at the back. "Now remember, we're saving this for the very last evening, so that you can wear it to the Grand Ball."

Emily took the opportunity to have a look at the other princesses. The girl nearest to her was the same one she'd seen getting out of the carriage earlier.

She had dark hair and serious brown eyes, and wore a green silk dress. She saw

Emily looking her way and smiled back.

The next girl stood gracefully with long golden hair falling down her back. Her mum was checking the fit of her pale-blue dress, which was so long that it even hid her feet.

The girl furthest away from Emily had dark eyes and wavy black hair. She wore a dress of bright yellow dotted with sequins. She saw Emily looking at her.

"Hi, I'm Lulu from the Kingdom of Undala near the Great Desert," she said with a wide grin.

"I'm Emily from Middingland," said Emily, smiling back. "It's great to meet you."

"I'm Jaminta, from Onica by the Silver River," said the girl in green.

"And I'm Clarabel," said the blonde-haired girl, smiling shyly. "From the Kingdom of Winteria in the cold North."

"When did you—" began Emily.

"Girls!" scolded Lulu's mum. "There'll be lots of time for chatting later. Stay still now, Lulu. We need to measure you for your velvet cloak."

"Thank goodness you mentioned that! I nearly forgot," said Emily's mum. "Every princess needs a cloak to wear at Mistberg Castle. Turn round, Emily, while I check how long it should be."

The princesses exchanged looks and grins as they lapsed back into silence.

Emily looked at herself in the mirror. The dress looked great already. She didn't really want to hide it under a cloak.

From outside the window came loud whoops and yells. Her mum was still holding the tape measure against her dress, so Emily tried to lean over to peer into the garden without moving her feet.

Right outside the window lay the

obstacle course that she'd seen from her bedroom tower. Now that she was on a lower floor she could see it much more clearly.

Four young princes were playing on the equipment, climbing the ropes, swinging across the monkey bars and flying down the zip-wire.

As Emily watched them, she longed to be out there. "Mum!" she burst out, trying to wriggle free. "Have you finished measuring for the cloak yet? I really want a go on that obstacle course."

"There'll be plenty of time for that later," said Queen Maria.

"Your Highness, we haven't given you all the necessary instructions yet," said the head dressmaker. "All young princesses must know the correct manners for the Grand Ball. How to enter the Banquet Hall and curtsy in the right place. How to hold your head straight as you walk along. How to place yourself on your seat correctly at the start of the meal. There are many things to practise this afternoon."

Emily sighed. The other princesses didn't look very happy either.

"I'm sure I know how to sit down on a chair," muttered Lulu. But she fell silent after a look from her mum, the Queen of Undala.

Emily looked from the zip-wire to her mum still fiddling with the tape measure. She sighed. It was going to be a *very* long afternoon.

Emily got back to her turret bedroom as the sun began to set. She found her maid, Ally, taking things out of her suitcase and putting them away.

Ally looked at her. "What's that frown

for?" she asked immediately.

Emily smiled. Ally had been her maid since she was five and could read her moods easily.

"We had to do lots of silly stuff, practising walking and curtsying and so on," said Emily. "Mum said I could go outside when we'd finished but there wasn't time, and now I have to go to the banquet. I'd really love to try out that zip-wire."

"Well, maybe you still can. If you choose the moment carefully, you could go out for a little while without them missing you," said Ally, picking up a pair of glittery silver shoes and putting them in the wardrobe.

Emily looked thoughtful. Ally always told her to work hard at her princess duties, but also liked her to think for herself. Everyone has a brain and everyone should use it, she always said.

Before she became Emily's maid, Ally had spent several years working as an undercover agent, solving jewel robberies and catching the thieves.

Emily sometimes wondered if her maid had really wanted to give up her old job, but Ally would just say that she was happy working in the palace.

"I know! I'll go out there after we've finished eating. No one will miss me just then," said Emily.

"Be careful," warned Ally. "And best take a torch with you; it's getting dark."

Emily put on a cherry-red dress for the banquet. She added a gold tiara and a gold necklace, which she'd been allowed to borrow from the dressmaking room.

Her heart began to thump faster. Now sitting and listening to the grown-ups' boring conversations wouldn't seem half as bad. She wouldn't mind the curtsying or the endless fussing with napkins. Not now that her own adventure was only a few moments away.

Chapter Three

Climbing in the Dark

Crystal chandeliers lit up the enormous Banquet Hall and rich tapestries lined the walls. Emily gazed round in amazement, her gold tiara sparkling on top of her red curls.

Over her dress she wore the black velvet cloak her mum had chosen for her. Her stomach rumbled as the delicious smell of roast dinner drifted through from the kitchens.

The kings and queens of the twenty

royal families from all around the world were bowing and chatting to each other. The Empress of the Marica Isles swept by, wearing a coral necklace that swung grandly from her neck.

The King of Undala, looking very noble in his golden turban, bowed low to Queen Trudy of Leepland, who gave him a sharp nod. At her side, she clutched a boy with a sulky mouth wearing an orange waistcoat.

Emily sat down at the banquet table next to her mum and dad. She knew who all the kings and queens were because she'd been studying them in her lessons for weeks. But she was thankful that she didn't have to start talking and curtsying to them all yet. The Grand Ball would take place in two days' time. Until then, she was happy to stay in the background.

"Emily, please remove your elbows from

the table," whispered her mum.

Emily took her elbows off and tried to sit up straight. It was harder than it looked. She gazed across the Banquet Hall and suddenly felt her shoulders tighten.

On a far table sat the man with the deep voice and purple hat who'd shouted at her earlier. Luckily he wasn't looking at her. He was smiling at the person sitting next to him, the twinkly eyed King Gudland. He didn't look so fierce now, although Emily still hoped she wouldn't run into him again anytime soon.

Queen Maria leaned towards her. "As well as meeting the other princesses, you'll see some princes here that are your age. Look, there's Prince Olaf of Finia."

Emily glanced at the tall, blond-haired boy from Finia, then she noticed the boy with the sulky mouth again.

"Who's the prince wearing orange, next

to the Queen of Leepland?" whispered Emily, wondering why he looked so grumpy.

"Mum? Why can't I have pudding first?" whined the boy. "You always let me at home."

"That's her son, Prince Samuel," said her mum quietly. "Now, remember, Emily! Use the cutlery from the outside first and chew slowly."

Emily stared at the huge spread of knives, forks and spoons next to her plate. *Use the ones on the outside first*, she thought. Why was there always so much to remember?

A gong sounded to signal the start of the meal. The food tasted wonderful, but Emily's feet tapped impatiently. When could she slip out? Did she have to wait until every single person had finished?

Finally dessert was served. Bowls of

treacle pudding and tall ice-cream sundaes were soon emptied, and the grown-ups began to murmur about having coffee in the drawing room.

Emily sprang up. "I'll be back in a minute," she said to her mum.

Queen Maria nodded. So Emily hurried away out of the hall, down the passageway and past the kitchens to the back door.

Her hand gripped the torch that she'd tucked underneath her cloak. Afraid of being caught at the last moment, she rushed straight out of the door and into the night.

She felt small in the darkness. Switching on the torch, she let the round beam of light travel over the garden. She tried to remember how everything had looked in daylight.

Over there were the fountain and the

maze. She followed the gravel path to a wide courtyard set out with chairs and tables. Then she hurried down a slope and there, beyond the lawn, stood the biggest obstacle course she'd ever seen.

She raced over to it, the beam of torchlight bouncing as she ran. Where would she start? The zip-wire, of course!

She shinned up the long ladder to the high platform and grabbed hold of the rope. The thought of flying down there in the dark gave her a bubbly feeling in her stomach, half excited and half scared.

She couldn't even *see* the other end of the wire; it was too far away in the shadows. Her skirts rustled around her as she got ready to leap off the platform.

Oh! She'd nearly forgotten! She couldn't go on the zip-wire wearing this huge cloak. It would only slow her down.

She pulled the cloak off and laid it

over the wooden railing behind her.
Then, taking the rope in both hands, she
jumped.

The darkness rushed past her. She
swooped down the wire, feet dangling, till
she felt the crash as the bar hit the other
end and her legs swung upwards. Then
she plunged backwards, slowing down
steadily until her feet hit the ground.

Emily let go of the rope, grinning
widely. She'd loved that; it was just like
flying.

"That was awesome!" A girl came
closer, her blonde hair and blue dress
glimmering in the light spilling from the
castle windows.

"Princess Clarabel?" asked Emily.

Clarabel nodded. "Yes, that's me.
I came out to look at the obstacle course.
I can't believe you went all the way down
there in the dark."

"It was brilliant!" said Emily. "Are you going to have a go?"

"I might." Clarabel chewed her lip. "Maybe I'll see how fast it goes first."

"Woo hoo!" The yell came out of the darkness.

Emily spun round, shining her torch into the air. A figure in yellow climbed up the cargo net and swung herself over the top.

"Princess Lulu conquers the world!" she shouted, scrambling down the other side.

Emily and Clarabel burst out laughing.

One last figure came running down the slope, a dazzling green light fixed to her arm. "Am I missing all the fun?" said Princess Jaminta.

Emily stared at her wrist. "What's that?" she asked.

Jaminta held out her arm to show Emily the bracelet that glowed far brighter than her torch.

"It's made of emeralds. I've found a way to make jewels work like gadgets," said Jaminta. "I can give them power or make them warm. Or I can make them light up just like this. I like using emeralds best."

"That's amazing!" said Emily admiringly.

"Ooh, I wish you could make my jewel glow," said Clarabel, touching the dark-blue sapphire that hung from a chain around her neck.

Lulu came running over, landing in front of them with a double-flip somersault. "I guess none of us could bear sitting still in that hall a second longer," she said, grinning. "So who's next on the zip-wire?"

"Let's race for it!" said Emily.

They raced to the ladder, laughing

as they ran. Lulu reached it first. She pulled herself up and the others followed. Climbing up last, Clarabel looked a little worried as she peered down at the ground.

When they all stood on the platform at the top, Emily said, "Shall we try going down it two at a time?"

But just then a noise came out of the night. A screeching sound that sent tingles down Emily's neck.

"What was that? It sounded horrible," exclaimed Lulu.

"That was a distress call," said Clarabel. "The sound of an animal in trouble."

"It came from out there in the forest," added Jaminta, shining her emerald bracelet in that direction.

"We should go and find it," said Emily. "We might be able to help."

"It's very dark," said Clarabel

nervously. "But you're right, some poor animal needs us."

"Let's go!" said Lulu.

The girls climbed swiftly back down the ladder and ran across the garden. They passed through the castle gates in a whirl of coloured dresses and rushed on into the forest beyond.

Chapter Four

The Dark Forest

Emily ran between the trees, glad that the other princesses were beside her.

It was much darker out here beyond the castle walls. Low branches reached down to catch them and Emily had to stop and untangle herself.

"Do you think we're going the right way?" she said.

"Listen," said Clarabel. "I think I heard it again."

They stopped for a moment, trying

to hear the animal noise over the wind blowing and the swooshing of the leaves.

"There it is," said Lulu.

The half-crying, half-grunting noise sounded much weaker now. The princesses ran towards it, slowing down as the ground became thick with tree roots and brambles.

On the earth lay a young deer with one leg bent at an awkward angle. The animal turned its black eyes on them, trembling with fright. Emily caught the glint of something silver on the ground.

"Look! It's caught in something," she said.

Clarabel knelt down next to the deer. "Poor thing! No wonder it made that horrible noise."

"That looks like a man-made trap," said Jaminta grimly.

"Why would anyone trap an animal

like this?" said Clarabel. "I'm sure it can't be allowed."

"King Gudland doesn't seem like the sort of king who would let this happen," agreed Emily. "How are we going to set it free?"

Jaminta bent down to look more closely at the metal teeth of the trap. The emeralds on her wrist cast a bright-green light over everything. Clarabel spoke soothingly to the deer, trying to calm down the shivering animal.

"The trap's clamped really tightly around its foot. It won't be easy to release it," said Jaminta. "And even if we manage it, the deer still won't be able to walk."

"Just get that trap open!" said Lulu. "I've got an idea." And she sprinted away through the forest.

Jaminta pulled a small screwdriver out of her dress pocket. "Could you keep its

leg really still?" she said to Emily.

Emily nodded and took hold of the deer's leg firmly, its brown coat feeling velvety beneath her hands. The creature quivered, its huge black eyes opening wide with fear.

"Don't worry," whispered Clarabel, stroking between its ears. "We'll have you free in no time." The young animal turned its soft nose towards her and its ears twitched almost as if it knew what she was saying.

Jaminta worked quickly, loosening four screws on the trap one after the other. The deer squirmed and Emily struggled to keep it still. She kept a tight hold on the leg, praying that Jaminta could work magic with her screwdriver and get the trap undone.

"Stay still, little one," murmured Clarabel.

Jaminta twisted the screws looser, one by one. "Nearly there," she said.

The deer wriggled harder and for a moment Emily thought she would lose her grip on its leg.

"That's it!" Jaminta pulled out the last screw and stuck the screwdriver behind her ear.

Emily pulled the trap open, keeping her fingers away from its sharp silver teeth. Gently she lifted out the deer's leg.

"Look! There's no cut here at all," she said. "Maybe this little deer just fell badly when the trap closed."

"Luckily it's young and its small leg fitted right between the teeth of the trap. Otherwise its injuries would have been much worse," said Jaminta.

Suddenly Lulu arrived, crashing through the branches with a wheelbarrow. "Great! You got the trap open," she said breathlessly.

The deer began shivering again, its wide eyes fixed on Lulu.

But Lulu didn't notice. "I found this in the greenhouse." She pointed at the wheelbarrow. "We can use it to take the deer back to the castle."

"We have to be really quiet though. It's still very frightened." Clarabel put her arms around the animal. "It's going to need a lot of looking after and it's going to take a while for that leg to mend."

"Let's lift it into the wheelbarrow – after three," said Emily. "One, two, three . . ."

They lifted the deer, which was surprisingly heavy, and set it down inside the wheelbarrow. Clarabel stroked the creature's soft ears until it became still and quiet, as if it sensed it was in good hands.

Emily and Lulu took one side of the

41

barrow each, while Jaminta and Clarabel
went on ahead, lighting the way with
Jaminta's glowing bracelet. They wheeled
the deer past the golden gates, into the
grounds and right up to the castle.

"Let's put the deer somewhere safe for
tonight and tell the grown-ups about it
in the morning," said Emily. "They won't
want to hear about it right now."

Clarabel nodded. "Good idea."

"There's a shed next to the
greenhouse," said Lulu. "It will be fine
in there."

Jaminta marched over to the castle
windows and peered in. "Looks like
they're still having their coffee."

Emily shrugged her shoulders. "They're
so busy chatting I bet they didn't even
hear the deer making that loud cry."

They settled the deer down in the
garden shed. Clarabel found some straw

for it to lie on and covered its legs with an old blanket that she found on a shelf. Lulu pulled some cabbages out of the garden and left them nearby in case it got hungry during the night.

The deer watched them, its big dark eyes no longer frightened. Finally it rested its head on one side and its breathing grew slow and steady.

Emily quietly closed the shed door and the four princesses looked at each other. Their tiaras glittered in the green light from Jaminta's bracelet and their eyes shone as bright as stars.

"I can't believe we went right out there into the forest in the dark," said Clarabel.

Lulu smiled. "And now you've got a leaf on your tiara."

Clarabel brushed off the leaf, then she laughed. "You've got a huge twig sticking out of yours!"

"Oops!" Lulu grinned.

Emily picked the twig off Lulu's tiara for her. Then she turned to Jaminta. "I think your bracelet's really clever."

"Thanks. I'd really like to make some more," said Jaminta. "I've got plans for what else I can do. I'll show you all tomorrow."

"Let's meet up before breakfast," said Lulu.

"Good idea. We should show King Gudland straightaway where we've put the deer," said Emily, smiling at her new friends. "If we tell him about the trap together, he'll have to listen. After all, princesses should stick together. No matter what."

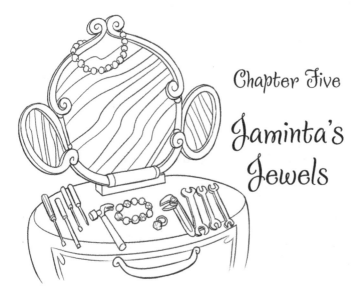

Chapter Five

Jaminta's Jewels

The four princesses dragged King Gudland down to the garden shed the following morning, telling him all about their deer on the way.

They had dressed quickly, throwing on dresses and plain silver tiaras. The morning sun beamed across the garden and made the tops of the castle turrets sparkle.

"We put it in here, Your Majesty," explained Lulu. "It seemed like a safe place." She pulled open the shed door to show the deer resting on its bed of straw.

"Goodness gracious!" said King Gudland.

"It needs some time for its leg to get better," said Clarabel.

King Gudland nodded. "Well, you've put it in the right place. It will be nice and peaceful in here."

"But why would anyone put out a trap for animals? It's such a horrible thing to do," said Emily.

"Trapping is forbidden in Mistberg Forest," said the king. "Perhaps it was just a branch that the deer tripped on. Perhaps you were mistaken?"

Emily's mum and dad arrived, having followed them across the garden.

"Girls!" interrupted Emily's dad. "Leave the king alone now. We haven't even had breakfast yet."

"But—" Emily wanted to mention the trap again, but the grown-ups were already turning away.

"Good morning, Your Majesties!" said a whiny voice. Prince Samuel, dressed in his orange waistcoat, walked over to them. He held a straggly piece of damp material out at arm's length as if it was something disgusting.

Emily looked at the material and her stomach lurched. She had a feeling there was something she'd forgotten. Something important.

"I found this at the top of the zip-wire," said the prince with a smirk. "I just wondered if it belonged to anyone."

"Emily!" cried her mum. "Is that your cloak?"

Emily grabbed the soggy cloak from the prince. "I must have left it there last night."

"Thank you, Prince Samuel," said Emily's mum. "Emily, I would like to talk to you!"

"Mum, you said I could go on the obstacle course," said Emily. "I just forgot about the cloak."

Queen Maria shook her head. "Of course you're allowed on the climbing equipment. Exercise is good for you. But honestly, Emily! You're not supposed to run off and play in the middle of a banquet!"

"I'm sorry," said Emily. "I only planned to be gone for a minute."

"You need to put your princess duties first. Remember what you should be doing and look after your belongings properly."

Emily sighed. "Yes, Mum."

The queen's face softened into a smile. "Now, let's go back inside. I hear the cook is serving blueberry muffins for breakfast."

Luckily the rest of the day was free from curtsying practice, although Emily had to take her sodden cloak down to the laundry room to be cleaned.

The princesses spent some time after breakfast feeding their deer. Then they gathered in Jaminta's room in the East Tower.

Jaminta's four-poster bed was hung with shimmering green and gold cloth. Her dressing table was covered with silver tools all neatly lined up, including a small screwdriver and a chisel.

"I can't wait to see these amazing jewels," said Emily.

"They're very special," replied Jaminta. "Where I come from, by the Silver River near the Eastern Mountains, we love to

collect precious stones. If you chisel them
into shape correctly, you can use them in
all sorts of ways."

She pulled the curtains across to
darken the room and put a large gold
jewellery box down on the bed. The other
princesses leaned in closer.

"These are the ones that give out light."
Jaminta carefully pulled back the lid.
Light burst from the shining jewels in all
the colours of the rainbow. They lit up the
dark room, making it seem like a cave full
of treasure.

"Wow!" cried the princesses.

"And now I'm trying to see what else I
can do with them. See!" Jaminta opened
a smaller jewellery box, picked out a
round ruby and put it into the palm of
Emily's hand. The jewel rested there,
gradually warming up until Emily felt like
she was holding a little ball of fire.

"It's so warm. It could definitely come in handy in winter," said Emily.

"That's good," said Clarabel. "It gets so cold in Winteria, where I come from."

"No need for extra heat in Undala," joked Lulu. "Our grasslands bake in the hot sun."

"Well, I haven't invented a jewel that cools you down," laughed Jaminta. "Not yet anyway!"

Clarabel smiled. "I don't think we would have found the deer last night without your bracelet. It was so bright."

"King Gudland didn't believe us about the trap, though," said Emily. "He thought we were mistaken."

Jaminta frowned. "It was definitely a man-made trap. It took me ages to get all those screws undone."

Emily looked thoughtful. "If the king doesn't believe us, then maybe we should go out and find the trap and bring it back to show him. Then he can look for the people who left it."

"Great idea!" said Lulu, and the others nodded.

"Let's hurry," said Emily. "The sooner we show the trap to King Gudland, the sooner we can prove that we were telling the truth about the deer all along."

Chapter Six

Meeting the Princes

Jaminta put away her jewels and
the princesses headed out into the
sunshine. On the way, they collected
King Gudland's dog, Denny, as they had
offered to take him for a walk.

They also charmed a picnic basket out
of the cook, stuffed with sandwiches,
slices of chocolate cake and a box of
strawberries.

As they walked across the garden, they
spotted the four princes playing on the

obstacle course again. Emily recognised Prince Samuel, the boy who'd handed her soggy cloak back to her that morning.

"Hey!" called the tallest prince. "What are you lot doing?"

"Going for a walk," Lulu yelled back, and the princesses kept on moving.

The tall prince, with a head of ruffled blond hair, ran over to them. "I'm Olaf from the Kingdom of Finia. Want to race against us on the obstacle course? Princes against princesses?"

Prince Samuel sniggered behind him. "That'll be easy. Princesses are *really* slow."

Lulu's eyes flashed. "You obviously haven't met princesses like us, then," she snapped.

"Are these your friends?" Emily asked Prince Olaf.

"Yes. This is George from Carathia."

Olaf nodded to a black-eyed boy, who grinned widely. "And this is Dinesh and he's from—"

"From Ratastan," said the short, serious-looking boy.

There was a pause and they all looked at Samuel.

"I'm Prince Samuel from the Kingdom of Leepland, the land of the most riches and the best people," said Samuel, his pale face twisting haughtily.

Prince Olaf ignored him. "So how about the race?" he asked the princesses.

Emily smiled. She'd never met any of the princes before, but she instantly liked the lively Prince Olaf. She wasn't so keen on Samuel, though; she was almost sure he'd enjoyed getting her into trouble earlier.

"Maybe we can race you later," said Emily, then paused. Should she mention their plan to find the deer trap? Maybe not in front of Samuel. "We're just taking King Gudland's dog for a walk."

She was about to add that they were going into the woods, when a shrill voice drifted down from the castle.

"Samuel! I hope you aren't getting that new waistcoat dirty!" The thin lady with the pointed nose trotted out of the castle door. "Samuel! What are you doing?"

Prince Olaf nudged Samuel. "It's your mum," he hissed.

Queen Trudy sped up, glaring at the girls as she came closer. "Samuel, I hope you're being careful who you're friends with. Just look at the mud on their shoes!"

Emily didn't want to wait around to meet such a bad-tempered person. She turned to the other princesses. "Let's go. We've got to get on with our walk."

They waved goodbye to the princes and headed off across the castle garden. Denny the dog bounded ahead of them. His tail wagged madly and the breeze ruffled his dark-brown coat.

"Denny! Come back!" shouted Emily, dodging round a stone fountain.

She chased him past a row of high fir trees, nearly running straight into the tall figure of a man. Darting sideways, she just managed to avoid him. But then she lost her balance, fell into a tree and got a face full of needle-like leaves.

"Aha! The red-headed princess! I was sure we would meet again," said a deep voice.

Emily recognised the man with the purple hat whose room she'd stumbled into the day before. Her heart sank. It was the worst luck to bump into him.

"It was so nice of you to drop in

yesterday," said the man, showing his teeth.

Emily assumed it was supposed to be a smile, but she couldn't help thinking of a shark. "I didn't mean to disturb you. I just went into your room by mistake," she said, jumping to her feet.

The other princesses came running up, and Denny darted round in circles barking at everyone.

The man showed a flicker of a frown when he saw the dog, but it was gone in an instant. "So where are you all off to?" he asked.

"We're going for a walk in the forest, My Lord," replied Lulu.

The frown returned. "That's not a good idea." The man paused. "It's so easy to get lost out there."

"That's OK. I have a compass to check our direction," said Jaminta, getting the

small round compass out of her pocket and showing it to him.

"Good day to you, My Lord," said Clarabel.

All the princesses curtsied and carried on walking across the garden.

The man didn't reply, but stood watching them, his dark eyes cast into shadow.

"Who is that?" asked Emily. "And why doesn't he want us going for a walk?"

"That's Duke Raven," Jaminta told them. "My dad told me that he lives in this kingdom and he's a cousin of King Gudland. Maybe he really thinks we'll get lost."

Ahead of them, the golden gates towered upwards, gleaming in the sunshine. This was where the castle grounds ended and the forest began. Clarabel put Denny's lead on to stop him running too far away.

They walked through the gateway and the trees stretched out in front of them. Shafts of sunlight drifted through the branches. Leaves rustled here and there as mice and squirrels scurried around.

"Which way to the place where we rescued the deer?" said Lulu.

Jaminta looked around and checked her compass. "We turned right just here. So we should be heading south-west."

They walked together, searching for any glimpse of metal on the ground.

"None of this looks the same as last night," said Emily suddenly.

"Well, it *was* really dark, even with the light from Jaminta's bracelet," Lulu pointed out.

"But there were tree roots everywhere and I can't see any here," said Emily.

Jaminta looked at her compass again.

"Maybe we should spread out a little more, but not so much that we can't see each other."

The princesses spread out through the trees and continued walking in the same direction.

Emily's stomach rumbled, which made her think about the chocolate cake in the picnic basket. Then her foot hit something and she grabbed hold of a tree trunk to stop herself falling over.

"Hey!" she yelled. "There are loads of tree roots over here."

The princesses came running up.

"Yes, this looks like the right place," said Clarabel. "Remember how the deer was lying right next to the bottom of a tree."

They searched all the trees nearby. Denny snuffled at the ground and wagged his tail excitedly.

"Look!" Clarabel pointed to a patch of earth with strange scrape marks on it.

Emily bit her lip. "Maybe this was the place. But where's the trap?"

Jaminta walked around the tree trunk, peering at the ground. She bent down next to a large footprint clearly marked in the soft forest earth. "Look at this," she said grimly. "Someone came here and took the trap away with them."

"That's terrible!" snapped Lulu. "First they set the trap and now they try to pretend it was never here."

"And we have nothing to show King Gudland," said Jaminta.

"They could come along with more traps and nobody would stop them!" cried Clarabel. "Then so many deer could get hurt."

"Wait!" Emily's face suddenly lit up. "Maybe *we* can stop them! I know a way

we can find out secrets. I know a way
we can move around the forest without
anyone ever seeing us."

"Really? How's that?" asked Lulu, her
lion-like eyes widening.

"We turn into ninjas!" said Emily.

The princesses' mouths dropped open.

"Really?" said Jaminta.

"Really!" said Emily. "We can be just
like ninjas and I know who can show us
how to do it."

Chapter Seven

Ninja Princesses

After checking on the deer in the shed and finding him some more food, Emily took the girls back to her room in the West Tower. The room had been tidied and the sofa scattered with soft red cushions.

"Hey! Ally's left slippers out for all of us," said Emily, wriggling her toes into the red slippers dotted with diamonds. "Almost like she knew we were coming."

She handed out the jewelled slippers

to her friends, green to Jaminta, yellow
to Lulu and blue to Clarabel. Then she
took one look at Clarabel's sad face and
sent an order down to the kitchen for hot
chocolate.

"I'm just thinking of the little deer,"
explained Clarabel. "What if he's missing
his friends? What if there are more traps
out there that we didn't see?"

Emily flopped down on to the sofa. "I
know," she said. "I've been wondering
the same thing. But Ally will help us find
out."

There was a knock on the door and Ally
came in with four steaming mugs of hot
chocolate and a plate of golden flapjacks.

"This is Ally, everyone," said Emily.

"Your Majesties!" said Ally, smiling. "I
saw you coming across the garden a few
minutes ago, so I sent another maid to
fetch those slippers. Is there anything else

that you need?"

"We need your help, Ally," Emily told her, taking a big slurp of hot chocolate. "We need to learn how to be ninjas."

"Emily!" warned Ally. "That was a long time ago and I don't talk about it these days."

"You can trust these princesses. Honestly you can!" promised Emily, and the other princesses nodded.

"Do you know lots of ninja moves?" Lulu asked eagerly.

"And did it take you long to learn them?" added Jaminta.

Ally pulled up a chair, her face serious. "Learning ninja skills takes lots of patience and hours of practice. But why do you want to know? What do you want to be ninjas for?"

"We think that someone's trying to trap the deer in Mistberg Forest without King

Gudland knowing about it," said Emily.

"But why?" Clarabel burst out. "Why are they doing it?"

"Maybe they want to catch a stag to take his antlers?" said Lulu. "That sort of thing used to happen where I live. Poachers came to trap animals for horns or antlers. We've driven those people out of our kingdom now."

"So you want to find out if there are more traps?" said Ally.

"Yes," said Emily. "And to discover who's leaving them."

Ally tightened her lips. "They're probably doing it at night so that no one sees them. It'll be dangerous out there."

"But if we can move around the forest without anyone seeing us, we'll be fine," said Emily. "We need to be ready to go out there tonight. Tomorrow's our last day here, the day of the Grand Ball. After that it will be too late. You will help us, won't you, Ally?"

Ally smiled. "Well, Your Majesties!" she said with a bow. "It just so happens that you've asked exactly the right person."

💜

Ten minutes later Ally and the princesses stood on the castle lawn. The girls had swapped their long dresses for sun tops and skirts in light colours.

Emily's pink top sparkled with silver thread and she'd pulled her red curls back into a ponytail.

"Don't we need to be camouflaged?" asked Jaminta.

"Not always," Ally told her. "I learned ninja skills from an old master when I trained as an undercover agent many years ago. You have to blend in wherever you are and whatever you're wearing. You have to be swift and cunning."

"So how do we practise?" said Lulu, keen to get started.

"Well, there's your target." Ally jerked her head towards the other side of the garden where the four princes were playing football. Prince Samuel's orange waistcoat lay on the grass near the goal. "Get that waistcoat and bring it back here without being seen."

"That's impossible!" declared Jaminta. "They're sure to see us."

"I'll go first! Let me have a try!" said Lulu, her eyes gleaming.

The other princesses sat down on the grass to watch. Lulu put on her dark sunglasses and sneaked towards the princes using the cover of nearby bushes.

She used her acrobatic skills, running and diving into a forward roll to keep herself hidden. But when she got closer the tallest prince saw her and waved.

Lulu came back, grinning. "I was so close! Who else wants a go?"

First Jaminta, then Clarabel tried to reach the waistcoat. But they, too, were spotted at the very last moment.

Emily's heart thumped faster. Silently she tiptoed over the grass and crouched behind a stone statue of a horse and rider. She peeked round the corner of the statue. The boys were only a short distance away across the grass but there was nothing else to hide behind.

How could she reach the waistcoat without being seen? Then she heard a snuffling behind her. Denny the dog was exploring the garden.

"Here, boy!" whispered Emily.

Denny came bounding over. She quickly searched for something to throw. There was a stick on the ground nearby. It was small, but it would have to do.

"Denny," she hissed, lobbing the stick high over the grass. "Fetch!"

Denny galloped after the stick, right through the princes' game of football.

Emily grabbed her moment. She sneaked across the grass, snatched the waistcoat and returned to the safety of the statue. The boys were too busy looking at Denny to notice.

"Well done!" said Ally approvingly as Emily returned with the waistcoat.

"I was lucky," laughed Emily. "I had some help from Denny!"

"A good ninja uses whatever they can find," said Ally.

Just then, the smell of sausages floated towards them.

"They've started the barbecue," said Ally. "Why don't I give you some more ninja training after lunch?"

"Great idea!" agreed Lulu.

But as the princesses walked over to the courtyard where the barbecue was cooking, a wail sliced through the air.

"My waistcoat! It's gone!" cried Prince Samuel.

Emily pulled a face. "Oh, I forgot! I'd better take it back." She ran across the lawn and handed the orange waistcoat over.

"What were you doing with my waistcoat?" moaned Samuel.

"Nothing, it's completely clean," said Emily. "Sorry, I didn't mean to upset you. I won't borrow it again."

Prince Samuel's face puckered like a squeezed plum. "Mother was right," he said. "You princesses are nothing but trouble!"

Chapter Eight

Moonlight in the Forest

By the end of the day the princesses had learned to spot good hiding places, to blend in with their surroundings, and slip in and out of rooms unseen.

The only mishap had been when Lulu crept into the kitchens and surprised the cook so much that he had dropped the gigantic raspberry jelly he was holding. It had splatted across the floor in a large wobbly mess. However, once the princesses had helped him clear up he had willingly forgiven them.

Emily smiled as she got ready for the evening banquet. The plan was a good one. They would sneak into the forest and hide there until they discovered who was laying the traps. Then they would tell King Gudland. Once he found out what was really happening, the deer would be safe again.

After a splendid dinner that the princesses were too excited to eat, they slipped out of the Banquet Hall one by one. Then they all gathered in Emily's room, having changed their ball gowns to dark tops and black velvet trousers.

"The trousers will be much easier to climb trees in," said Emily. "Is everyone ready?"

"Yes!" said Lulu and Jaminta.

Even Clarabel nodded, although she looked a little pale.

Four princess shadows flitted down the stairs and out of the back door by the kitchens. They reached the golden gates for the second time that day and paused. The moon shone down, turning the forest a beautiful silver.

"We must stay together all the time," whispered Emily.

The others nodded.

They walked stealthily towards a huge oak tree, avoiding twigs that would crack and snap, the way Ally had shown them.

Emily had noticed the oak tree earlier that day. It had branches low enough to climb up on and plenty of room to hide four princesses.

Pulling themselves up, they climbed from branch to branch. Then they tucked their legs in carefully and prepared to watch and listen unseen.

Jaminta's bright emerald bracelet lay

deep inside her pocket. Everything had to stay completely dark.

For a long time, there was nothing. Just the hooting of an owl and the scuffling of a little creature on the ground. Lulu shifted impatiently.

"Stay still," hissed Jaminta. "You're wobbling the whole branch!"

Then far in the distance, a tiny light bobbed up and down. It disappeared for a moment and then returned again. As it grew bigger, they heard the rhythm of footsteps and the murmur of a voice.

The princesses froze like little mice when a wolf passes by. At last the light came close enough for them to see its owner. Two dark figures walked along together, stopping here and there to put something down on the ground.

"They're setting more traps," whispered Emily.

79

The two figures crunched closer, grumbling as low branches caught their heads. They stopped right underneath the princesses' oak tree.

The girls held their breath.

"How many more do we have to do?" said a man's voice.

"Two more," replied another man. "Then we've put down all ten of them."

Emily let out a gasp, then covered her mouth with her hand. She remembered seeing the men before.

"Did you hear that?" said one man.

"Hear what? Nothing's coming near us while you're stomping along like a great elephant," said the other. "Come on."

It seemed like forever until the men moved away. When their light had disappeared completely, the princesses clambered down and dropped one by one on to the soft earth.

"We have to find King Gudland right now!" said Clarabel, her face pale. "Loads more deer could get trapped."

"I've seen those men before," said Emily. "They were the ones inside Duke Raven's room when I went in there by accident."

"Ready everyone?" Jaminta got her emeralds out of her pocket to light the way. "Watch your feet! Those traps could snap shut on us just as easily as on a deer."

They ran as fast as they dared, back past the golden gates and into the castle garden. Long shadows streamed behind them in the moonlight.

Quickening their pace, they sped over the lawn, across the courtyard and through the back door, reaching the entrance to the Banquet Hall, hearts drumming and breathless.

The Banquet Hall was empty, the plates and dishes from dinner already cleared.

"They must be in the drawing room," said Lulu.

They raced across the Banquet Hall and down another corridor towards a closed door.

"Who goes there?" Two guards in red uniform stepped forward, blocking their way.

"We're the princesses," said Emily. "We need to speak to King Gudland." In her black velvet trousers and with no tiara, she suddenly realised she didn't look very much like a princess.

"All the kings and queens are taking part in the royal council meeting," said the second guard. "No one is allowed in."

"But we must go in!" insisted Lulu. "The Mistberg deer are in danger. There are traps in the forest."

"Please let us," begged Clarabel.

But the guards shook their heads. "Sorry, our orders are to let no one in until the meeting is over."

"But when will they be finished?" asked Emily.

Jaminta answered her. "Not for ages, I bet. My dad says those meetings go on till late into the night."

The princesses trailed back down the corridor to the Banquet Hall.

"We can't give up now. We're princesses," said Emily simply.

"We'll just have to sort it out ourselves," said Lulu, putting her hands on her hips.

They paused, thinking hard.

"I know how to make some deer noises," said Clarabel. "I can mimic their danger call to warn the deer away from where the traps are."

"And I worked on some new jewels

this morning," said Jaminta. "They're diamonds that light up like magic when they're close to metal. We can use them to find the traps quickly."

Emily's eyes sparkled. "And we've got our ninja moves."

"And our acrobatics," added Lulu.

"We can do this! Let's go!" said Emily.

The princesses raced to Jaminta's room to collect the new jewels: a handful of diamonds that sparkled like stars.

Then they sprinted faster than ever towards the forest, their only thoughts for the safety of the deer. No one wanted to say it, but they all knew that the next trapped deer could be seriously hurt or even worse.

They skidded to a stop in front of the golden gates.

The gates were closed. A huge gold padlock held them tightly together.

"What's happened?" gasped Emily. "They were open a minute ago."

A shadow stepped out from behind a nearby statue. "I don't think princesses should be wandering around in the forest," said a deep voice. "They might get in my way."

The moon came out from behind a cloud and shone down on the man's face and his purple hat.

Emily's stomach lurched as she recognised who he was. "Duke Raven!" she groaned.

"Yes," said the man with a nasty smile. "I made the servants lock these gates to keep you nosy girls out of the forest. There's no way you will get in there now."

Chapter Nine

Trapped

"I watched your little game on the lawn this afternoon," Duke Raven continued. "And I knew you were going to interfere with my plans."

"But we're only trying to help the deer," said Clarabel.

Emily stared at the duke. "Your plans! So that's why we saw those men in the forest. You sent them in there. You're the one trying to trap the deer. Why would you want to do such a terrible thing?"

"Deer antlers will look delightful on my palace wall," the duke sneered. "And when I've chosen the best pair for myself, I'll sell the rest. Mistberg Forest deer have the most beautiful antlers in the world. They'll make me an awful lot of money." His narrow eyes glittered.

"We'll go and tell King Gudland what you're doing," said Lulu.

"He'll never believe you. I'm his cousin, and you've got no proof. Without that, he'd never believe anything bad about me."

And with an air of complete satisfaction, Duke Raven strolled back across the lawn towards the castle.

"Now what?" cried Lulu, shaking the gates angrily. They clanged loudly, but the padlock held them shut.

"Is there another way to get into the forest?" asked Emily.

Jaminta shook her head. "I don't think so. This is the only way out of the castle grounds. Unless we can climb the fence."

Lulu tried to haul herself up the wooden fence, but slipped down again straightaway.

"It's too high and too slippery," said Clarabel.

"We need something to climb up on," said Jaminta.

Lulu's eyes gleamed. "How about each other's shoulders?"

"Do you really think that would work?" said Emily doubtfully. "We've never tried it before."

"I don't like being high up, but I'll try anything to help the deer." Clarabel's face was pale but determined.

So they arranged themselves next to the fence and climbed unsteadily up on to each other's shoulders. Lulu, as the tallest, went at the bottom, followed by Emily, then Jaminta. Clarabel, as the shortest, was meant to climb past them all to reach the very top.

"This is terrible!" she cried, after falling off for the seventh time. "I just can't balance."

Luckily the grass underneath gave her a soft landing.

"Why don't I have a try?" said Emily, and, after a lot of wobbling, she managed to scramble past Clarabel to the top of the fence. Pushing her hair out of her eyes, she leant down and pulled Clarabel up. Then between them, they hauled up Jaminta and finally Lulu.

They had chosen a place where a sturdy tree branch stretched across to the fence on the forest side. So one by one they shinned along the branch and down the tree trunk to the ground.

"Phew!" said Emily, as she landed on the forest earth. "I guess Duke Raven wasn't expecting us to do that."

"Duke Raven is a bad man," said Lulu stormily, and the others agreed.

They picked their way through the forest, directed by Jaminta's compass and the light from her bracelet. Then a rustling up ahead made them stop.

Something moved. It stepped into a shimmering shaft of moonlight and stood there, its antlers transformed into silver.

"Look," breathed Emily. "It's a stag."

The beautiful animal turned its head towards her, listening.

"Are we ready?" said Clarabel. "I'll make the danger call to scare it far away."

They all nodded.

Clarabel lifted her hands to her lips and made a series of high-pitched noises.

The stag caught the sound and galloped away, his hooves echoing through the trees.

"It's working! Keep going, Clarabel," said Emily. "We'll find the traps."

Jaminta quickly handed out diamonds to Emily and Lulu, and the three of them scoured the forest floor, waiting for the diamond to light up when it found any metal.

"Here's one!" cried Emily. Her diamond glowed, shedding its light like a forest star.

Jaminta rushed over and showed her how to spring the trap, making its deadly jaws close round a stick.

"Once the trap's sprung it's useless," she explained. "It can't hurt an animal after that."

They rushed from place to place, hunting down the traps in the darkness.

Each princess worked fast. The silence was broken only by the snap of closing traps and Clarabel's deer calls ringing eerily though the forest.

Emily felt as if her diamond was leading her through the trees, as if it knew where she needed to go.

Each time it lit up a little brighter, and Emily sprang the trap and rushed on, trailing diamond-light behind her like star dust.

As the hint of a pink sunrise peeped through the trees the princesses gathered around their oak tree again.

Sleepiness was starting to cloud over Emily's eyes, but she gave herself a shake. This was no time to lose concentration.

"How many traps have you found?" she asked.

"Two," replied Lulu.

"Three," said Jaminta.

"And I've found four. That makes nine altogether," said Emily. "That means there's only one left to find."

"That's great!" yawned Lulu. "It can't be far away. Let's carry on."

They spread out again. Emily walked along staring so hard at her diamond that she didn't even notice where she was going.

At last the sparkling stone glowed white. Emily grinned. She'd found the very last trap!

A rustling made her look up. She was standing in a forest glade full of flowers and thick grass. Deer grazed quietly all around her, and there, right in the middle, lay the trap.

Emily froze. The deer were everywhere, full-grown ones and babies. Any sudden movement or noise could make them run and one might run straight into the trap.

The thought of hearing it snap shut on the deer made Emily shiver inside. She turned, as slowly as she could.

"Clarabel?" she croaked. "Where are you?"

The deer raised their heads, poised to run.

"I'm right here, Emily," answered Clarabel. "I'll wait for your signal."

Step by tiny step, Emily edged towards the trap. If she could get to it, then maybe she could stop the deer coming any nearer. She could keep them safe.

As she got closer, she could see how well the trap was hidden in the long grass. "Clarabel? Now!" she called softly.

Clarabel let out the deer's danger call and the animals took flight, galloping away through the trees.

Emily felt relief flood through her. She grabbed a stick and sprang the trap. Its teeth snapped tight shut like a metal crocodile.

"We've done it!" said Clarabel.

Emily picked up the closed trap and glared at it. "This is the one we're taking to show King Gudland. It's time that he knew what's been going on."

Chapter Ten

The Grand Ball

Ally brought a feast of pancakes and golden syrup up to Emily's room that morning. The girls were absolutely exhausted. Spending the whole night saving deer was hard work, even for a princess.

So they sat round the little table, wearing gold-trimmed dressing gowns and tiaras, munching pancakes and drinking tall glasses of peach juice.

King Gudland had been astounded

when they gave him the trap, and shocked to hear that Duke Raven had shut the castle gates to try to stop them carrying out the animal rescue. Emily hadn't realised that his twinkly eyes could turn so cross.

"Thank goodness for you four brave princesses. I would never have believed it of Duke Raven if you hadn't shown me this horrible thing," he'd said, turning the trap over. "There will be no more traps in Mistberg Forest. I will sort this out once and for all." And then he had marched angrily away.

Shortly afterwards, Duke Raven's carriage sped down the driveway and out of the castle grounds. The duke's face frowned from the carriage window.

"Look! Duke Raven's leaving," cried Emily, leaning over to look out of her turret.

"I bet King Gudland's thrown him out of the castle," said Jaminta.

"Good! That saves me having to do it!" said Lulu, taking another pancake and a large helping of syrup.

The others giggled.

The rest of the morning was spent down at the shed, looking after the deer with the injured leg and finding vegetables for him from the kitchens.

In the afternoon, a feeling of excitement swept through the castle as the decorations went up ready for the Grand Ball. People rushed up and down the stairs with banners, golden tablecloths and enormous bunches of roses.

Every dress was smoothed, every shoe was polished, and every ring, bracelet and necklace rubbed until they sparkled.

The princesses met up in Emily's

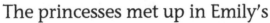

room in their ball gowns. The orchestra downstairs had already started to play, and the melody drifted right up into the West Tower.

Emily checked her smooth pink satin dress in the mirror. Then she put on her ruby necklace, a ruby ring and her best tiara which was shaped like golden leaves woven together.

She turned to the others. "You know, we make a really great team."

"That's because we're really good at animal rescues!" said Lulu. "We're Rescue Princesses!"

The other princesses smiled.

"There must be loads of animals around the world that need our help," said Clarabel.

"You're right," Emily agreed, her hazel eyes shining. "If only we could get together to save them. But how can we call on each other? We won't be together all the time."

Jaminta looked thoughtful. "Maybe there is a way. I haven't tried it out yet, but I have an idea that could help us."

Just then, a trumpet fanfare sounded. The ball was about to begin. They climbed down the spiral stairs to the Banquet Hall together. Emily's long red curls bounced as she stepped downwards and her pink dress with its red flowers shimmered in the light.

She glanced at her friends, looking perfect in their ball dresses and tiaras. No one would ever have thought they'd used ninja skills or scrambled over the castle fence the day before.

Jaminta wore a straight dress of dark-green silk decorated with beautiful golden thread. An emerald necklace hung around her neck and she had brushed her dark hair till it shone. Perched on her head was a tiara bejewelled with beautiful Onica crystals.

Clarabel had to be careful not to tread on her pale-blue dress, which had a wide skirt right down to her toes. Her golden hair hung loose and a sapphire gleamed around her neck, matching the sapphires in her tiara.

Lulu wore a shorter dress of bright yellow dotted with sequins, and a necklace with a beautiful yellow topaz. She stepped down the staircase swiftly, her black hair braided into tiny plaits and pinned up beautifully under a bright, golden crown.

Emily's stomach began to gurgle as she climbed downwards. There were so many people that she would have to greet and curtsy to.

The room below was crowded with

kings and queens from all twenty royal families. They wore ceremonial robes and cloaks in every shade from the brightest red to the deepest blue.

Suddenly the orchestra seemed deafening and dozens of crowns glinted in the dazzling light of the chandeliers. Emily took a deep breath and carried on down the staircase.

As the princesses reached the bottom, the four princes – Olaf, George, Dinesh and Samuel – came to stand next to them. They were also old enough to be presented at this year's Mistberg Ball.

The kings and queens began to form two long lines, taking the younger princes and princesses to stand with them. Emily watched a little princess, maybe only four years old, clinging to her mother's hand as she moved to her place in the line.

When the kings and queens were

ready, two long lines of royalty stretched out from the staircase. The princesses exchanged a look. This was the moment they had practised for.

They would have to walk between those lines and curtsy and speak to every single grown-up. They had to show that they could act exactly the way a princess should.

Emily took a deep breath and stepped forward. The first person in the line was a tall king with a beard. Emily curtsied. The king bowed.

Emily's heart rose as she went down the line. Everyone was smiling, she realised. The very last person in the line was King Gudland. When Emily had curtsied, he took her hand.

"Princes and princesses, kings and queens," he said loudly. "May I have your attention?"

Everyone fell quiet. The other princesses came to stand next to Emily.

"We are very proud of all our young people. But I have something special to say about these four princesses."

He smiled at Emily. "We can see that these young ladies walk and curtsy beautifully. But today they proved that they have much greater talents than this. They showed us how to be brave, inventive and kind to other creatures. They have saved many deer from terrible harm. I can only say how grateful I am to them, and how delighted I am to have them here. They will always find a warm welcome at Mistberg Castle!"

The kings and queens burst into applause.

"Now," continued King Gudland when the clapping finished, "let the Grand Ball begin!"

The orchestra struck up a fast tune, which sent Emily's feet tapping. She and the other princesses danced and laughed under the sparkling light of the chandeliers.

Trays of strawberry juice and fizzy cherryade were brought around, together with plates of iced cupcakes decorated with sugar crowns.

Emily noticed Prince Samuel trying to take five cupcakes before Queen Trudy pulled him away. Emily twirled and swirled until her head felt light and her feet tingled.

She smiled to see King Gudland joining in. He even tried to teach them his favourite dance move, called "The Mistberg Funky Chicken".

Prince Olaf came past, jiggling to the music. "Hey! So did you really rescue all those deer?"

"Yes, we did!" replied Emily.

"That was really brave," said Olaf. "Want to dance?"

"Maybe later," smiled Emily, twirling away towards her friends.

"Emily!" said her mum, taking her to one side. "Your dad and I wanted to say how proud we are of you. You did well telling King Gudland about those traps, and you've made some lovely friends. We must ask the other princesses to come and visit Middingland soon."

Emily beamed. "Thanks, Mum! I'm sure they'd love to!"

At last all the cherryade had been drunk, and Emily's feet grew tired. As she went to say goodnight she saw Jaminta whispering to Lulu and Clarabel.

"What is it?" she asked.

"Can I borrow your ring? Just for one night?" murmured Jaminta.

"Of course," said Emily.

Jaminta winked. "I'll show you why tomorrow. I want it to be a surprise."

Emily took off the ruby ring with its jewel that shone like fire and gave it to her friend. She yawned. With a successful animal rescue and an exciting Grand Ball, this really had been the best day ever!

Chapter Eleven

The Rings and the Promise

Emily wanted to check on the little deer before she left the next day. When she reached the garden shed she found Lulu, Jaminta and Clarabel already inside.

"Look!" said Clarabel. "Isn't it amazing?"

The deer tottered towards Emily, holding steady on its injured leg. Its soft brown ears pricked up as it listened to the girls, and its tail twitched.

"That's great! He's so much better,"

said Emily, delighted.

"I've asked the gardeners to look after him when we go home," said Lulu. "And they'll take him back to the forest next week, when he's completely better."

"There's one more thing," Jaminta said, taking a velvet bag from her pocket. "Last night you all lent me your rings and I worked really hard on them."

She handed the sapphire ring back to Clarabel, the yellow topaz to Lulu and the ruby to Emily. Then she put on the emerald ring.

Emily slid her ring back on to her finger. The jewel in the middle had changed just a little. It was heart-shaped and it shone with a deeper fire. "Can they do something special now?" she asked.

Jaminta looked pleased. "It took me a long time, but I managed to make it work. Now they are communication rings. So if you speak into yours we'll all hear you, no matter where we are and no matter how far away."

"Wow!" said Emily, her eyes wide.

"Thanks, Jaminta," said Clarabel.

Emily twisted the ring on her finger. "You know, there'll be lots more animals out there that need our help. We should make a secret promise to always help an animal in trouble."

"No matter how dangerous it is!" added Clarabel.

Lulu grinned. "The more danger there is, the better!"

"And now we have the rings, we can get help easily," said Jaminta. "We can call each other straightaway."

"And no one else will know that we're really Rescue Princesses!" said Emily.

The girls stood in a circle with their hands joined in the middle, one on top of the other.

"We promise to help all animals in trouble," said Emily.

"We promise," said the others.

The four rings glowed for a moment and Emily's heart missed a beat. Their adventures had only just begun.

The Rescue Princesses
The Moonlit Mystery

Paula Harrison

nosy
crow

For Teri, who was there on the journey

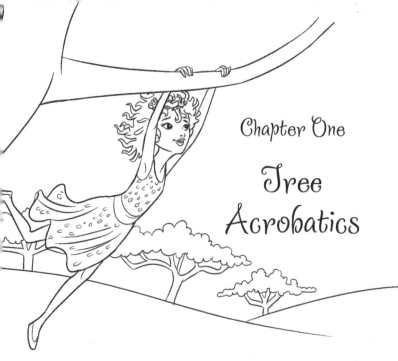

Chapter One

Tree Acrobatics

Princess Lulu grasped the lowest branch of the tree with both hands and swung herself backwards and forwards. After a few swings, she stretched high enough to curl her legs right round the branch above.

Her wavy black hair swayed as she climbed. She wore a short yellow dress dotted with tiny golden beads. It was her tree-climbing dress and it was now extremely dusty. On her left hand she wore a ring with a gleaming yellow topaz, her favourite jewel.

Halfway up the tree, there was a long straight branch, almost as straight and smooth as the beam in her gym. She loved practising in the gym, but being out here with the sun blazing down and the breeze on her face was even better.

On her left stood the palace of Undala with its courtyard and fountain, and on her right was the outer wall, with the golden grasslands beyond. In the distance, an elephant lifted its trunk at the waterhole, getting its early morning drink.

Lulu smiled and turned back to the branch in front of her. She wanted to see if she could do a cartwheel along it. She stood tall and gazed straight ahead, excitement fizzing inside her. Then, pointing one foot, she raised an arm high

above her head, ready to cartwheel.

"Atchoo!" The ear-splitting sneeze came from below, making Lulu jump. She wobbled and nearly fell off the branch. Grabbing hold of the tree trunk, she peered down at the ground.

Prince Olaf stood under the tree, his spiky blond head looking up at her. Lulu sighed. Olaf was visiting the Kingdom of Undala with his parents, the King and Queen of Finia, and ever since arriving he'd been following her around. He'd seemed so nice when she'd met him before at royal balls and banquets. But now she thought he was a know-it-all!

Olaf sneezed again. "Sorry!" he said. "I was just watching. I love learning acrobatics and circus skills. I was practising them in your gym yesterday. Maybe I can teach some to you?"

Lulu swung down from the branch and

landed on the ground in front of him, hands on her hips. "You were practising in *my* gym?"

"That's right." Olaf grinned, not noticing Lulu's frown. "And I think I'm getting really good at walking the beam."

"Really?" Lulu folded her arms. "How many times did you fall off, then?"

"Oh, a few times." Olaf didn't look even the tiniest bit embarrassed. "Would you like me to show you how to do it? I can always hold your hand if you're nervous."

Lulu's eyes flashed. Olaf was the most annoying, puffed-up prince she'd ever met! "No thanks!" she snapped. "I can turn hundreds of cartwheels on my beam and I certainly don't need anyone to hold my hand!" She was about to add that she would show him just how good she was, but the low clang of the breakfast gong interrupted her.

Lulu rushed inside with Olaf trailing behind her. She was going out to the grasslands with Walter the ranger this morning and she didn't want to be late. She bounded into the palace hallway, with its shelves of beautiful animal carvings. A huge painting of a lion standing at the foot of a mountain hung next to the doorway. Inside the Great Hall, the maids were setting out the breakfast plates. Lulu hurried in and found a seat at the long wooden table.

"Good morning, Lulu. Good morning, Olaf," said Lulu's mum, Queen Shani, with a warm smile. "Have either of you seen Lady Malika?"

Lulu shook her head and helped herself to the warm buttered rolls.

"No, I haven't, Your Majesty," replied Prince Olaf, with a sweeping bow. "But I'll go and look for her if you like."

Lady Malika was the queen's sister who lived on the other side of Undala. It was a long way away, so she didn't visit them very often. She owned a big circus in the city which Lulu had visited once when she was little. Like the Finians, Lady Malika had come to stay at the palace for a few weeks.

"Thank you, Prince Olaf. But there's no need. I just wondered where she was as I noticed that her room was empty," said Queen Shani. "Perhaps she had something important to do this morning, so she left the palace early."

Lulu scowled at Prince Olaf, who was offering the bread rolls to her mother politely, and wished more than anything that her friends, Princesses Emily, Clarabel and Jaminta, had come to stay instead. She knew they'd love Undala, with its huge grasslands filled with wild animals. She sighed wistfully, just as a horn tooted loudly outside the window.

"That's Walter! He must be ready to leave," she cried, racing out of the hall and down the front steps.

"Slow down, Lulu! Must you rush everywhere?" the queen called after her.

Lulu jumped into the truck next to Walter, who smiled at her. "Let's go!" she cried.

They zoomed away between the tall palace gates, with the red earth flying beneath their wheels.

Chapter Two

Princess of the Wild

Walter drove them across the rough grassland, circling carefully round a herd of grazing elephants. "I suppose you want to see the lioness's hollow again?" he said, pushing up the sleeves of his checked shirt.

"Yes please!" Lulu's dark eyes shone in delight. "Maybe today the cubs will come out to play."

Walter slowed the truck down in front of a patch of bushes, before coming to a stop underneath a tall tree.

"I'm going to check the animals at the waterhole," he told her. "Remember what I said about staying in the truck. It's not safe for you to walk around on your own."

Lulu nodded. But as soon as he'd disappeared down the slope, she leapt up from her seat as if waiting one more second would make her burst. She grabbed hold of the lowest branch of the tree above her. Hauling herself up, she reached for the next branch and the next, climbing swiftly. At last she stood at the very top and the beautiful Kingdom of Undala spread out below her.

Miles of tall golden grass rippled in the wind and in the distance the black-and-white blur of a zebra herd moved slowly across the plain. But Lulu wasn't interested in zebras. She'd seen them hundreds of times. Her eyes were fixed on a hollow in the sun-baked red earth. A bush right next to the hollow quivered and a small paw stuck out.

Lulu grinned in delight and crouched up on her branch, hanging on to the tree trunk with one hand. She'd been waiting for this moment for six long weeks, ever since the lioness had made the hollow into her den. She knew all about the animals that roamed near her palace and she knew that the cubs would be nearly ready to come out for the very first time. She was so excited at the thought of actually seeing them!

A low growl came from the hollow and the lioness sprang into view. She padded out of the bush, sniffing the air in all directions. Satisfied that there was no danger near, she settled down on the dusty earth and gave another growl. Five little lion cubs skipped out of the hollow,

bounding all around their mother. Their golden fur gleamed in the sun. The smallest cub struggled to climb up on to his mother's back. He slipped off over and over again, but finally managed to scramble up and fell straight to sleep at the top.

Lulu smiled as she watched them. Five cubs was a really good-sized litter and they were so cute. She settled more comfortably on the branch, until footsteps below reminded her that she hadn't come here alone. Walter was shading his eyes as he looked up into the tree.

Lulu waved to him, clambered quickly back down and dropped into the seat of the truck.

Walter got into the driver's seat and drove off jerkily. "I thought you were going to wait in the truck. It can be dangerous out here," he said.

"I know, I'm sorry, Walter," said Lulu. "But don't worry. I didn't walk around, I just climbed right up the tree. And guess what?" She grinned at the ranger happily. "The lion cubs came out to play and there are five of them!"

Walter grunted. "But you could have fallen out of the tree. What would the king and queen say?"

"I'd never fall out!" said Lulu, laughing. "It's a really easy tree to climb and it was worth it to see the little cubs. Thanks for letting me come with you."

Walter grunted again and looked at her from under his bushy eyebrows. "You didn't just come along to avoid that prince, then?"

Lulu looked at him solemnly. "It was all about seeing the lion cubs, I promise you."

Walter snorted with laughter and swung the truck round. As the royal ranger, he looked after a vast area of grassland and animals. Lulu knew that he liked her company on the long drives. But he was also right that she was glad to get away from Prince Olaf.

Later on, she would write and tell the other princesses all about the cubs. Together, the four girls had made a secret promise always to help any creature in trouble and had already performed two daring animal rescues. Lulu missed her friends very much and she knew they'd love to hear about the baby lions. She so wished they could see the cubs for themselves.

"We're driving round to the other side of the waterhole next," said Walter. "I need to check the number of hippos living there. After that we'll have a look at how far the bison herd has moved."

❤

They spent a long day driving around checking the numbers of animals in the area and making sure that they all looked healthy. As the sun dipped in the sky, they headed back towards the palace for dinner.

"Could we please have one more look at the lion cubs?" begged Lulu. "Just for a minute."

"All right, then," said Walter. "As it's on our way."

They stopped underneath the tree near the lioness's den. The orange sun was setting now and the bushes next to the hollow were completely still.

Walter took out his binoculars and peered through them. "That's strange," he said. "There's no sign of them at all."

Lulu took the binoculars and had a

look. "I'll climb the tree again. I can see the whole den from the top." She swung quickly up the tree, but even from there she saw no glimpse of the lioness or the cubs.

Frowning, Walter climbed out of the truck and walked towards the bushes. He peered over them for a few moments. Then shaking his head, he returned to Lulu. "It looks like they've gone," he said.

"Gone?" repeated Lulu. "You mean they've moved to another den?"

"Maybe. But . . ." His frown deepened. "There have been far fewer animals around here lately. There aren't as many zebras or leopards as there should be. I haven't seen them leave. It's almost as if they've just disappeared."

"Why would they disappear?" she asked, but Walter shook his head again.

Lulu felt a cold dread grow inside her.

Surely nothing bad had happened to the cubs? Surely the lioness would have protected her babies from danger?

Just then there was a faint cry, almost like a cat meowing, and a scrabbling noise came from behind a rock. Lulu's heart thumped. What could be hiding there? Was it an animal in trouble?

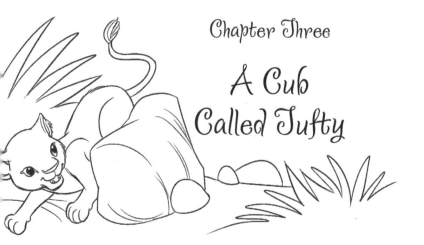

Chapter Three

A Cub
Called Tufty

Forgetting all about the danger, Lulu
jumped out of the truck and raced over to
the rock. Hiding behind it was one little
lion cub, with sticking up fur on his ears.
He looked at her and gave a mournful
yowl. Lulu thought he had the most
beautiful brown eyes she'd ever seen.

"You poor little thing!" she said to the
cub. "Are you all alone?"

The cub mewed and lifted up one paw.
Lulu turned to Walter with a

determined look in her eye. "We have to take him back with us," she said firmly. "He's too young to manage on his own." She picked up the tiny cub and stroked him soothingly.

Walter raised one bushy eyebrow. "If you take him, he'll be your responsibility until we find his family. Do you really want to feed him and look after him?"

"Of course!" cried Lulu.

"And where will you put him?"

"He can sleep with me in my bedroom, that way I can look after him really well."

Walter sighed and gave in.

They wrapped the lion cub up in a blanket and he rode back to the palace on Lulu's lap. He squirmed a lot, his ears stayed pricked up and his inquisitive little eyes watched the grassland rushing past him.

"I'm going to call you Tufty," said Lulu,

scratching the sticking up fur on his ears. Tufty gave a deep purr and nudged Lulu's hand, closing his eyes blissfully.

The truck slowed down as they approached the gates and the high tangerine walls of the palace came into view. Behind the palace loomed the huge black shape of Shimmer Rock, the only mountain in the Kingdom.

When she got inside, Lulu sneaked Tufty up to her bedroom still hidden under the blanket. She knew her parents wouldn't like her looking after the cub, but she was sure he was too little to be dangerous. She wasn't going to tell Prince Olaf, either. He was bound to run and tell the grown-ups. Oh, how she wished the other Rescue Princesses were here!

She set the little cub down on her bed and he scampered across her duvet, trying to catch a fly with his tiny paws.

The fly got away and Tufty rolled over on to his back, waving his legs in the air like he was pretending to swim.

Lulu chuckled. "You're so funny! I know Emily, Clarabel and Jaminta would love you so much."

Tufty rolled back on to his tummy and looked at her with big brown eyes.

She stroked his furry ears. "I bet you miss your brothers and sisters, but don't worry. I'll look after you. Everything will be all right. Walter and I will find your family as soon as we can."

But that evening brought some bad news. Lulu was tiptoeing through the hallway to the kitchen to fetch milk for Tufty, when one of the kitchen maids walked past and saw her.

"Oh, good evening, Your Majesty!" The maid bobbed a curtsy. "Walter asked me to give you this." And she handed

Lulu an envelope.

Lulu tore it open and read:

Dear Princess Lulu,

I've been called away for a few days to work on the other side of Undala, near the Great Desert. Take good care of the lion cub. He'll need milk every few hours. And remember not to fall out of any trees!

With all my best wishes,

Walter

Her heart sinking, Lulu climbed back upstairs. She sat down in front of the mirror and stared at the streaks of reddish dust on her face. Who was going to help her find the missing lions now?

She heard soft padding paws behind her. Tufty let out a low meow, leapt into her lap and curled up, purring.

"Oh, Tufty!" she said. "I forgot your milk!"

But Tufty just closed his eyes and purred. With a sudden ripple of excitement, Lulu knew what she had to do. She didn't have to sort this problem out all alone. It was time to call the other Rescue Princesses! They would find the lions together.

She looked in delight at the yellow topaz ring on her finger. Each of the four princesses had their own ring made from a different kind of jewel. But they weren't just ordinary rings. The princesses could use them to call each other for help with an animal rescue. Jaminta had shaped the jewels perfectly to bring out the magic inside them.

Lulu smiled. Now she could find the missing lions *and* see her friends again. She lifted the ring to her lips, pressed the yellow topaz and spoke clearly into the jewel.

"Calling all Rescue Princesses! This is Lulu in the Kingdom of Undala. There are animals in trouble here. I repeat: there are animals in trouble."

The yellow topaz glowed brightly for a second. Then a voice came from far away. "This is Jaminta in the Kingdom of Onica. I'm on my way to help you."

"Hello, Lulu," came a second voice. "This is Clarabel in Winteria. I'll set off as soon as I can."

There was silence. Lulu waited hopefully.

"This is Emily in the Kingdom of Middingland." The third voice sounded very faint. "I wouldn't miss another rescue for anything!"

The yellow topaz glowed once more and the voices were gone. Lulu beamed. She felt like turning hundreds of cartwheels all round the room. But Tufty was sleeping peacefully on her lap, so she contented herself with giving his soft ears another stroke.

"The Rescue Princesses will be here soon," she whispered to him. "They'll come as fast as they can." Her heart thumped with excitement.

Then she was struck by a sudden thought. How was she going to tell her mum and dad that she'd invited her friends to the palace, and that they were already on their way?

Chapter Four

A Noise in the Night

Lulu frowned hard, trying to work out what she was going to say to the king and queen. How could she tell them that she needed her friends to visit without giving away their secret? She had to think fast.

Lifting up the sleeping lion cub, Lulu laid him down carefully on her pillow and sneaked out of her room. There were lights on downstairs, so her parents were probably still awake. She hurried down, determined to persuade them to let her friends stay.

The Great Hall was empty but there were voices outside in the courtyard.

"It's difficult running a circus." Lady Malika's voice was sharp. "It's hard to find new acts that people want to watch."

"Yes, but I think using animals would be the wrong thing to do," said Queen Shani quietly. "A circus really isn't a suitable place for a wild animal to live."

Lulu took a deep breath and marched into the courtyard. Her parents and Lady Malika were sitting next to the fountain, enjoying a cup of Undalan tea.

"Goodness, Lulu!" laughed Lady Malika. "You're up late!"

Queen Shani rose from her seat, her silver crown glittering. "What's the matter? Are you feeling ill?"

Lulu shook her head. "I wanted to ask you something important."

"You're very dusty!" Lady Malika's eyes narrowed. "Have you been out into the grasslands today?"

"Yes, I went in the truck with Walter to check on the animals," Lulu replied.

"What was it you wanted to ask, Lulu?" said the king, his golden turban gleaming in the lamplight.

"I'd like you to invite my friends, Princesses Emily, Clarabel and Jaminta to visit us soon." She hesitated. "Actually, I, er, sort of already told them they could come." She crossed her fingers and hoped her parents wouldn't ask exactly how she'd invited them. She really couldn't give away how the secret rings worked.

"Lulu!" exclaimed Queen Shani. "You really must think a little harder before you rush off and do things like that. Now I shall have to telephone the other kings and queens to explain."

Lady Malika stared at Lulu, her head tilted to one side. "Sister!" she said. "Maybe it would be a good idea to invite these girls to stay. Then they can do princess things together, rather than roaming around the grasslands."

Lulu stared back at Lady Malika. She was grateful that her aunt agreed with her. She just wasn't sure why her aunt had spoken up like that. It was hard to tell what Lady Malika was thinking behind the sharp eyes and half-smiling mouth.

The queen's brown eyes were thoughtful. "Well, it would be nice for you to have some friends here," she said at last. "As long as their parents are happy to let them come."

"I'm sure they'll come if you send a proper Royal Invitation, sister," said Lady Malika.

The king and queen exchanged looks. "All right, then," said Queen Shani. "The other princesses can come."

"Thank you!" cried Lulu.

The queen raised her hand to quieten her daughter. "But only if you promise us something in return."

"Anything!" said Lulu, her dark eyes lighting up. "I'll do anything."

"The princesses can come as long as you are nicer to Prince Olaf," said the queen.

Lulu groaned. Being nice to Olaf would be really hard work.

"And we want you to take some lessons with Madame Rez," added the king.

"What? Why? Who is she?" said Lulu.

The queen sighed. "Do try to speak gently, my dear."

"But who is she?" said Lulu.

"Madame Rez is your new deportment

teacher," said the king. "She's here to help you learn proper princess manners."

Lulu pulled a face. That all sounded extremely dull, but what choice did she have? "All right, then, I'll be nice to Prince Olaf and do the new lessons." She dropped a wobbly curtsy.

Bouncing back upstairs, she forgot all about the tricky promises to her parents. The important thing was that the other princesses were coming and together they would find Tufty's family.

She was about to climb into bed when she heard a noise outside. Padding over to the open window, she looked out into the darkness. The moon was hidden but the stars made a pattern across the sky like scattered jewels. She began to turn away, when a glint caught her eye. Something winked at the far side of the garden, next to the old grey wall near the gardener's shed.

Holding the fluttering curtain still, she stared hard at the spot. But nothing else happened. Maybe it had been a firefly or the eyes of a lizard?

Lulu gazed at the little lion cub curled up on her bed. His soft tummy rose and fell as he breathed quietly in his sleep. "Don't worry, little Tufty," she whispered. "The Rescue Princesses are coming. We won't let you down."

Lying her head on the pillow, she closed her eyes and thought of Emily, Clarabel and Jaminta. The sooner they got here, the sooner all the lions would be back together and happy once again.

Chapter Five

The Royal Banquet

Lulu hovered by the palace gates, her heart thumping. She scanned the dusty road for any sign of a carriage. All she'd seen so far were gazelles leaping across the grasslands. The queen had sorted out the invitation muddle on the telephone, and Emily, Clarabel and Jaminta had all flown to the Undalan airport that morning from their different countries.

Lulu wished her dad had sent a car to fetch them, but he wanted them to have a proper royal welcome.

"All visitors must be greeted by the royal carriage, Lulu," he said. "We can't just send some silly car. It would be wrong."

"It would be faster," said Lulu.

The king smiled and shook his head.

At last, a speck appeared in the distance and grew larger.

Lulu leapt up and down, her eyes sparkling. "They're nearly here!"

A golden carriage, driven by two horsemen in purple uniform, drew up to the palace gates. Three heads leaned out of the carriage window, one red, one black and one golden.

"Hey, Lulu!" called the princesses. "We're here!" And they waved to her madly.

"I'm so happy to see you!" shouted Lulu, waving madly back.

At last, the carriage stopped at the

palace steps and three princesses climbed out eagerly. They were followed by Ally, Emily's maid, who had come to look after them.

"Welcome to the Kingdom of Undala," said Queen Shani, smiling at them all.

Emily's red curls bounced as she dropped a curtsy. "Thank you, Your Majesty. I bring good wishes from the Kingdom of Middingland."

"We're so pleased to come and visit," Clarabel said shyly, her blue eyes and blonde hair sparkling. "I also have good wishes, from the land of Winteria."

"My greetings come from the Kingdom of Onica. Thank you for inviting us," added Jaminta, her straight dark hair falling to her shoulders.

Lulu jumped up the palace steps, bursting with energy. "Great! Now that's all finished, come this way, girls."

"Just a moment," said the king, laughing. "The princesses must be introduced to our other visitors, then there will be a royal banquet to celebrate their arrival."

Lulu sighed. Banquets always took so long. She just wanted to talk to the princesses in secret and start making a rescue plan.

"We'll have time to catch up later," said Emily, winking at her.

"Right, later!" Lulu grinned and winked back.

So after they'd been introduced to everyone, the princesses went upstairs to put on their best ball gowns and favourite tiaras. Lulu longed for them to meet Tufty, but she knew she would have to wait until after dinner. They met in the hallway next to the huge lion picture and waited for the dinner gong to sound.

Emily wore a pink satin ball gown, while Clarabel's was pale blue and shimmered in the light. Jaminta wore a dress of wonderfully smooth green silk. Their special rings sparkled on their fingers. Emily's ring was a red ruby, Jaminta's was a green emerald and Clarabel's was a sapphire of the deepest blue.

Lulu's golden tiara matched her golden dress, which swished around her as she moved. Her yellow topaz ring twinkled. She grinned at her friends. "I've got so much to tell you," she said. "I hope dinner doesn't take too long."

"I got here as fast as I could," Emily told her. "I begged my parents to let me pack as soon as your message came through!"

"The rings worked really well," said Lulu, smiling at Jaminta. "Prince Olaf asked me why I wore mine all the time, but I wouldn't tell him."

"We saw lots of animals through the carriage windows," said Clarabel. "I've never seen giraffes before. They're so tall but so graceful."

"But which animal is in danger, Lulu?" asked Emily. "You didn't tell us in your message."

Lulu's face clouded over. "A lioness and four of her cubs have gone missing. No one knows why. Walter, he's the palace ranger, thinks other animals have disappeared, too. Something really strange is going on."

"What's really strange?" said Prince Olaf, coming down the stairs.

Lulu scowled and nearly said something cross. Then she remembered her promise to her parents. With a huge effort, she turned to Olaf. "It's strange that the banquet hasn't started yet, that's all."

Just then, the kings and queens and
Lady Malika arrived, dressed in their
smartest robes and crowns. The King and
Queen of Finia had fair hair, just like
Olaf, and wore velvet robes that hung
down to the floor. Lady Malika wore a
long black dress and her hair
was decorated with bright feathers.

"Good evening, Your Majesties!" Prince
Olaf swept them a huge bow, giving them
all a close-up of the top of his spiky blond
head. "And good evening, princesses."

The princesses bobbed a curtsy.

The Queen of Undala nodded
approvingly. "You have lovely manners,
Prince Olaf."

Lulu rolled her eyes. Why couldn't her
mum see how annoying Olaf was?

The gong sounded for dinner and
they all trooped into the Great Hall. The
long table was laden with delicious food

served in golden dishes. Lulu, who had been too excited about seeing her friends to eat very much, suddenly realised how hungry she was. She grinned as Emily sat down next to her and groaned inwardly as Prince Olaf sat down on the other side.

"I'd love to go and see some wildlife tomorrow," said Olaf loudly. "I thought I saw a squirrel earlier and it'd be great to see some more."

Lulu rolled her eyes again and took a huge bite of dinner so that she didn't have to reply. Did he seriously think squirrels lived in Undala?

"Actually, we don't have any squirrels in our country," said Queen Shani. "But it's a lovely idea for you to see the wildlife. I'm sure Lulu will take you."

Lulu shot a look of dismay at the other princesses. The last thing she wanted was to be stuck with Olaf when there were animals to help!

"You must go to look at Shimmer Rock as well," said the King of Undala. "There are stories about the mountain going back hundreds of years."

"What do the stories say?" asked Emily.

"Shimmer Rock is supposed to be a hollow mountain with magic inside, so the old tales go. And it shimmers in the moonlight, just like its name says. People used to think the lights were pixies having a party in the night." The king chuckled at the thought of it. "Of course, it's all made up. But the place is still worth a visit, after all, it's the only mountain in Undala."

Lulu sighed, all this talking was just slowing things down. But she perked up as bowls full of sweet Undalan trifle were brought round for dessert. The trifle was made from juicy chunks of mango and mouthfuls of cream. Lulu smiled and scooped it up quickly. Trifle was her favourite.

The King of Finia leaned forward. "I hear that you run a circus, Lady Malika. That must be very exciting. Our son, Olaf, is interested in acrobatics."

Lady Malika nodded. "It keeps me busy. There's always so much to do."

"I once heard of a circus that had performing elephants," interrupted Olaf.

The princesses stared at him in shock. How could people make wild animals do tricks in a circus? It was horrible.

"We don't have animals in the circus in Undala," said Queen Shani. "It isn't allowed. But we like acrobatics and clowns very much."

Lady Malika frowned a little and helped herself to more trifle.

Lulu stifled a yawn. The kings and

queens could be talking for ages. "May we go now?" she asked.

Queen Shani nodded, so the four princesses curtsied and hurried up the stairs, their dresses swirling as they climbed. When they reached Lulu's room, a scratching noise from behind the door made Emily, Jaminta and Clarabel back away, wide-eyed.

"Don't worry!" said Lulu, grinning. "It's just a friend of mine. He's staying here for a while."

"Really?" said Clarabel nervously.

Lulu gently swung the door open and there was the lion cub, his eyes shining and his whiskers quivering. He sprang over to Lulu, twisting in and out of her legs and purring.

Lulu saw her friends' surprised faces and laughed. "Girls! I'd like you to meet Tufty."

Chapter Six

Tracking the Lions

Lulu told the princesses how she'd secretly brought Tufty to the palace after the other lions had disappeared. Then Emily, Clarabel and Jaminta cooed over him, all wanting to stroke him at the same time.

The little cub became quite excited with all the attention and started leaping on to the bed and jumping off again, sending the girls into fits of giggles. At last, Clarabel, who seemed to soothe him the best, managed to settle him down with some warm milk in a baby's bottle from the kitchen. After that he snuggled down on her lap, still wide awake but quiet.

"It's a good thing he's such a young cub. Those claws will become sharp in a few weeks' time," said Jaminta.

"I think he's lovely!" Clarabel squeezed him tight. "But you're right, Jaminta. He's still a wild animal and he'll need to be back with his family soon."

"So where shall we look for them?" said Emily.

Lulu sighed. "I don't know. The hollow where they lived is empty. There's no sign of them at all."

Emily pushed back her red curls. "Maybe we can go back there and look around for clues. I've heard that tracking is an important ninja skill. Why don't I ask Ally if she can show us how to do it?"

Lulu sat up straight, her heart beating faster. "Great idea! Let's take Ally out with us tomorrow morning."

All the princesses trusted Emily's maid, Ally, completely. She'd helped them manage animal rescues before and would never give away their secrets. As well as being excellent at polishing tiaras and cleaning ball gowns, Ally also had unusual skills from her previous job. Before she began working at the palace in Middingland, she had been an undercover agent who caught jewel thieves. The princesses had used the ninja skills she'd taught them several times.

So, early the following morning, the princesses tiptoed down the stairs. A faint orange light had just begun to seep into the dawn sky and the palace lay completely silent. The four girls sneaked into the kitchen and gathered bread rolls and juice for their safari breakfast. As they crept through the hall, Clarabel accidentally bumped into the enormous dinner gong. Only Lulu's speedy dive to grab it stopped the whole palace being woken by a deafening chime.

Stifling their giggles, the girls ran out to the truck where Ally was sitting. Then she drove them quickly towards the palace gates.

"Duck!" hissed Lulu, as they passed the front entrance.

The princesses crouched down in their seats, making themselves as small as possible. The gates passed by on either side and they drove out into the wilderness beyond.

"What happened? Why did we have to hide?" asked Jaminta, climbing back up on to the seat.

"It was Prince Olaf." Lulu grimaced. "He was staring at us from an upstairs window."

Emily looked surprised. "Does it really matter if he saw us?"

"My parents wanted me to take him out to see the animals, remember?" said Lulu gloomily. "He'll ruin everything if he comes along."

Clarabel tucked her golden hair behind her ears. "Don't you like Prince Olaf, Lulu? I've always thought he was quite nice."

"He seems quite cheerful," added Emily.

"You don't know how awful it's been," Lulu said darkly. "Every time I do something, he's there, trying to do it first. He thinks he knows everything. And the other day . . ." She paused for effect. "He said he'd been playing on my gymnastics equipment!"

The other princesses burst out laughing.

"You're funny, Lulu!" said Emily. "It sounds like he's just trying to be friends with you."

But Lulu shook her head. "I'm so glad you're here now. Prince Olaf was driving me mad!"

They stopped for a moment to let a herd of zebras gallop past, then they drove on across the rough ground. The sun rose higher in the sky. Soon they reached Lulu's tree, right next to the lion cubs' hollow.

"This is the right place." Lulu swallowed a lump in her throat as she thought of the little cubs playing together. "There were five cubs and a lioness. Then, when I came back later, there was only Tufty left."

Ally told them to look around carefully with binoculars before leaving the truck.

Once they were sure that no wild animals were prowling nearby, they got out and walked over to the hollow.

"Are these the lion paw prints?" asked Jaminta, looking closely at some marks in the earth.

Lulu crouched down. "These are the cubs' prints and these are the lioness's," she said, pointing them out.

She followed the paw prints through the thick bushes and out the other side, right up to where the trail met long swathes of golden grass. She called out to the others, her heart thumping. "Look, everyone! The tracks lead away from the den right into the grassland!"

Chapter Seven

Manners and Mischief

"Can you still see the tracks under all that grass?" asked Clarabel.

Lulu waded in. "It's a little bit harder, but I can still see them."

"One moment, Your Majesties," said Ally, crouching down in the hollow. "See these tracks? They're really close together." She walked along the trail. "And here the paw prints get further and further apart."

"What does that mean?" said Emily.

Ally stood up, shading her eyes with her hand. "When the tracks get further apart, it means the animals started to run."

"Maybe they ran because something scared them?" said Clarabel.

Lulu called to them from the long grass. "Look at this! The tracks go up to here and then they just stop. There's nothing else."

The others rushed over to look.

"You're right, they do just stop," said Jaminta. "I wonder why."

They all stared at the last set of paw prints, half-hidden by the grass. Even Ally shook her head.

"Poor cubs! At least there's no sign they were hurt," said Clarabel.

"But how did they just vanish?" cried Emily. "It doesn't make any sense."

Lulu scanned the horizon, tears

pricking behind her eyes. Giraffes were nibbling leaves from the treetops. An elephant stood by the water hole. But there were no lion cubs.

"I hope we can find them," said Clarabel.

"We *will* find them!" said Lulu fiercely. "Rescue Princesses never ever give up."

Climbing back into the truck, Ally and the princesses used a map of the grasslands to plan out where to search. Then, hot, tired and covered in red dust, they drove back to the palace. Lulu was having her first lesson with her new deportment teacher after lunch and Ally insisted she shouldn't be late.

Lulu frowned as she changed out of her comfortable dress and put on the one she was supposed to wear for the lesson. It was a wide-skirted ball gown that hung down to her ankles. She stared at its frilly edges in the mirror. She liked shorter dresses better. This one would be totally useless for turning somersaults.

The lesson began downstairs in a room next to the palace courtyard. Madame Rez was a skinny, grey haired lady who looked Lulu up and down through little round glasses. Then she made her practise standing up and sitting down over and over, telling her each time what she was doing wrong.

"To be really ladylike, you must have good manners. Hold your skirt like this," said Madame Rez, lifting one corner of her long gown. "And then place one leg behind the other as you carefully lower yourself to a seated position."

Lulu sighed, grabbed her dress and plonked herself on the chair.

"No, no, no!" Madame Rez clutched her face in horror. "Those are not the manners of a princess! Keep your back straight and lift the skirt delicately like this."

Lulu grimaced and pulled her tiara down over her forehead. She knew she should try harder but it seemed such a waste of time. She longed to get back outside and carry on the search for the lions. She sat down on the chair, swinging her legs and looking out of the window.

"Next we will practise how to sit still on a chair," declared Madame Rez.

Lulu groaned.

By the end of an hour, she still hadn't managed to sit down and stay still in a way that made Madame Rez happy. She felt cross and hot, and just about ready to leap out of the window.

"Let us try standing straight by balancing a book on the head," said Madame Rez. "There is so much I must teach you, to make you ladylike!"

Lulu's mouth dropped open. She'd already lasted an hour, surely it was time to stop! She had to find a way to make Madame Rez let her go.

Just then there was a faint scratching at the window which looked out on to the courtyard.

"What was that?" said Madame Rez sharply. "We cannot have any interruptions."

The scratching grew louder and a deep purring made the window pane rattle.

Lulu swung round to catch a glimpse of big, brown eyes and whiskers pressed up against the glass. Then the creature's mouth opened to reveal two rows of large, pointed teeth.

Chapter Eight
Tufty finds a Hiding Place

"A wild beast!" shrieked Madame Rez. "There's a wild beast outside!" And she scurried out of the door in a surprisingly unladylike manner.

Lulu giggled. She ran over to the window and opened it to look for Tufty. She spotted Clarabel, who was holding the wriggling cub in her arms.

"It's all right, she's gone now!" hissed Lulu. "You can come out."

Emily and Jaminta, who had been

hiding round the corner, came over to join Clarabel.

"Sorry, Lulu!" said Jaminta. "Tufty slipped out of the bedroom when we opened the door."

"We had to chase him round the palace," added Clarabel. "Luckily no one saw us."

"Sorry to spoil your lovely lesson!" Emily grinned.

Lulu rolled her eyes. "It was terrible! I felt about as ladylike as a giraffe! Now let's get out of here before someone spots Tufty."

Lulu slipped out of the door and beckoned them to follow her. But just as they were about to hurry away, they heard footsteps coming towards them.

"Where shall we put Tufty?" whispered Clarabel.

Lulu looked around, but there was

nothing in the hallway that would hide a wriggly lion cub. Then an idea struck her.

"Pass him to me," she said, taking Tufty from Clarabel's arms. Quick as a flash, she put him down on the floor and swung her skirts over him so that he was hidden underneath. Luckily her long, frilly dress reached right down to the ground. She dropped her skirts just as Lady Malika swept around the corner.

"What are you all doing?" she asked, looking at the girls with narrowed eyes.

"Nothing," said Lulu.

"Really, nothing at all," added Emily.

Tufty gave a little mew beneath Lulu's dress, which Jaminta tried to drown out with a loud cough.

"It's nice to see you in a proper dress for a change, Lulu," said Lady Malika.

Lulu's skirts shook as Tufty bounced around underneath, trying to find a way out. "Er . . . thank you, Aunt," she said.

Lady Malika frowned for a moment. Then she gave them one of her half-smiles and walked away down the corridor.

"That was close!" whispered Emily.

Picking up Tufty, Lulu raced away, with the others following close behind.

♥

After taking the little lion cub back to Lulu's bedroom, the princesses hurried out in the truck to search the grasslands again. But to their disappointment, there was still no sign of the lioness or the missing cubs.

As the sun began to set, they returned to the palace to eat dinner with the grown-ups and Prince Olaf. Afterwards they gathered in Lulu's room, wearing pyjamas. Their jewelled rings glimmered on their fingers. It was a hot night and

the windows were flung wide open to try
to catch any faint breeze.

"If only we'd found some kind of clue,"
sighed Lulu, folding up the map of the
grasslands.

"Let's try again tomorrow," said
Clarabel. "We'll find them somehow."

There was a knock at the door, and
Ally entered carrying a tray of sugared
marzipan sweets shaped into little flowers
and stars. The girls settled down on Lulu's
bed to eat the sweets. After his afternoon
of mischief, Tufty had fallen fast asleep.

Ally crossed to the window to close the
curtain, but dropped it with a gasp when
the full moon came out from behind
a cloud. As shafts of moonlight hit the
mountain, its enormous black shape
began to shine until the whole peak
transformed into glittering silver.

"What's wrong, Ally?" Lulu leaned

forward. In the moonlight she could see that Ally was quite pale.

Ally stared at the mountain. "So that's why it's called Shimmer Rock! I'm sorry, Your Majesties," she smiled weakly. "It made me think of something from long ago."

"Why does Shimmer Rock sparkle like that, Lulu?" asked Jaminta.

"Well, the stories say that there's magic in the mountain," said Lulu. "But if you go right up to it and look closely, you can see millions of tiny crystals inside the stone. The moonlight makes the crystals shine."

"What is it, Ally? You look so strange!" Emily peered at her.

Ally hesitated. "I've heard about this mountain before," she said slowly. "Although I didn't know then that it was called Shimmer Rock. It all happened when I was working as an undercover agent searching for the missing Onica Heart Crystals."

"I remember you telling us about them before," said Emily. "You said they're the most famous missing jewels in the world!"

"And they were the most prized treasure in my kingdom, a long time ago," added Jaminta, who came from Onica.

"That's right. They were very famous and highly prized jewels," agreed Ally. "I was told that they'd been crafted out of gems which came from a 'land of lions', but it was a secret exactly where that was. Now I think that maybe it was here."

"Those Heart Crystals must be very beautiful," said Clarabel.

"Maybe jewels could help us find the missing lions?" said Lulu excitedly. "How about your pearl, Clarabel? Remember

how you used it to find the dolphin last time? Maybe you could use it to find the lions."

Clarabel shook her head. "It's an ocean gem, so it only works for ocean creatures. Are there any other jewels that we could use, Jaminta?"

The princesses all looked at Jaminta hopefully. She had great skill at shaping gems to give them a special power, a skill she had learned from a master gem maker at home in the Kingdom of Onica.

Jaminta pulled a velvet bag from her pocket, opened it and poured a handful of glistening jewels on to the bed. "I can't think of anything that would help us. Here's the amethyst Clarabel chose from the treasure chest on Ampali Island. All I've done is polish it so far." She picked up the purple jewel and then yawned widely. "But looking at it always seems to make me sleepy."

The other three girls looked at the sparkling purple jewel and yawned too.

"How strange that a jewel should make us so sleepy!" Emily said, rubbing her eyes.

Ally took one last look at Shimmer Rock and closed the curtain. "Maybe you'll have some new ideas in the morning, Your Majesties. For now, I think you should get some sleep." She went to pick up the sweet tray but accidentally knocked it on to the floor with a clatter.

The noise woke Tufty, who jumped up in the air, landed on the floor and scrambled under Lulu's frilly ball gown which was lying in a heap. The dress rippled as he disappeared underneath it.

"Don't worry, Tufty. Everything's all right," said Lulu, with a grin.

At the sound of her voice, Tufty stuck

his whiskery nose out of an arm hole,
making the princesses burst out laughing.

Lulu scooped him up and kissed him.
"Come on, little one. It's time for bed."

Chapter Nine

Night Ninjas

But Lulu couldn't get to sleep that night. Through the open window came the buzz of insects and the distant yowl of a leopard. She kept thinking about the lion tracks and the empty hollow where the little cubs had lived. She shut her eyes tight, but sleep didn't come. It didn't help when Tufty jumped up on her bed and started nuzzling her cheek and purring deeply into her ear.

"Tufty!" she laughed, pushing him off.

"Are you trying to tell me you're hungry again?"

Tufty padded up and down the blanket, still purring. So, with a wide yawn, Lulu threw off the covers and climbed out of bed. She crept down the dark stairs and felt her way towards the kitchen. Everyone was in bed and all the rooms lay in quiet shadow.

Lulu filled the baby's bottle up with milk from the refrigerator and fastened the lid back on. She smiled; this would stop Tufty feeling hungry for a while. Turning to hurry back upstairs, she caught a glimpse of light through the window. It was round and yellow in the darkness.

Running to the window, Lulu looked out into the blackness.

A full moon turned the garden a shadowy silver. Beyond the high palace wall, Shimmer Rock glittered brightly.

Lulu stared hard at where the light had been. She saw it again, right over by the old grey wall next to the gardener's shed.

Suddenly, she realised that she'd seen a light in the same place from her bedroom window two nights ago. What could it be? Was it someone with a torch? Nobody should be out there in the garden. The palace guards always stayed by the gate and everyone else was asleep.

She set the bottle of milk down on the kitchen table, her heart beating like an Undalan drum. Something strange was happening out there in the darkness. She dashed towards the stairs. It was time to wake the Rescue Princesses and find out exactly what was going on!

❤

The princesses slipped into light cotton dresses and plain silver tiaras, and crept silently down the corridor. A loud snoring came from Olaf's bedroom. Lulu looked at her friends and, trying hard not to giggle, they sneaked away down the stairs and out into the dark courtyard.

"Where are we going?" whispered Emily.

"This way," hissed Lulu, leading them through an archway at the far end of the courtyard. Beyond the orange trees was the vegetable patch and behind that was the high wall that surrounded the palace grounds.

"It really is such an amazing mountain!" said Clarabel, gazing at Shimmer Rock as it sparkled.

But Lulu had seen the mountain like that a thousand times and hurried them on towards the shed. "The light came from right over here," she said.

Jaminta tried the shed door but it was

locked. "There's nothing here, Lulu. Are you sure you weren't dreaming?"

"Totally sure!" Lulu walked right up to the shed. "There used to be a huge pile of things here." She pointed at the ground on one side of the shed. "There were wheelbarrows, spades and sacks of earth. But everything's been moved."

She stepped forward and her foot made a dull thud against the ground. She stopped, surprised.

"What was that?" said Clarabel nervously.

Lulu moved her other foot, which made a thudding noise too.

"That's strange. It sounds really hollow," said Emily.

Kneeling down, Lulu swept her hand across the ground and found that the loose earth moved aside easily beneath her fingers. She kept on brushing it away until she reached a solid rectangle of wood set into the ground.

"I didn't know there was anything under here," she cried. "It's always been covered up with gardening tools before."

"Not too loud," breathed Clarabel. "You'll wake the palace."

Jaminta knelt down beside her and tapped gently on the wooden rectangle. "It's like a door lying in the ground." She brushed more earth aside to reveal a ring handle made of metal and a small hole for a key. "Look! Here's the door handle and the lock."

"If it *is* a door, then let's open it," exclaimed Lulu.

"Shouldn't we figure out what it is first?" said Clarabel.

Lulu was already yanking on the handle. The door gave a huge creak but held firmly shut.

"Let's all try pulling together!" said
Emily.

So all the princesses took hold of the
ring handle and heaved as hard as they
could. But the door wouldn't budge.

"We need the key," said Lulu. "But who
would have it? No one knows this door is
here."

"Someone must know," replied Jaminta.
"And I bet the person with the key is the
same person you saw with a light."

Lulu stared round the garden. There
was no sign of the light any more. "I
don't know who that could be. No one's
ever talked about this."

She broke off suddenly. A strange noise
came from below the wooden rectangle,
making them jump.

"What was that?" said Emily.

Lulu crouched right down and put
her ear against the door, and the other

princesses did the same.

They waited for a moment, silent in the darkness. Then the noise came again from deep down, making the door shiver.

The princesses jumped to their feet.

"There's an animal down there!" gasped Clarabel.

"It's a lion," said Lulu, her eyes wide. "That's the sound of a lion's roar."

Chapter Ten

The Door in the Ground

The princesses looked at each other in excitement.

"Maybe it's our missing lions!" cried Emily. "But why would they be underground?"

"We'll have to go down there and find out!" Lulu tugged on the handle again, but it wouldn't budge.

"I know something we can use to unlock it," said Jaminta. "Come on!"

The four girls raced back through

the moonlit courtyard into the palace. Jaminta stopped in the kitchen, searching through the cutlery drawer. "It looks like quite an old lock. So maybe we can open it with a long piece of metal without needing the right key." She drew out a fork with wide prongs. "This might do it."

The other princesses crowded round to look.

With a sudden click, the light went on, dazzling their eyes. They swung round in shock to find Prince Olaf standing in the kitchen doorway. He was wearing stripy pyjamas that were so big the sleeves hung right over his hands.

"Hello," he said, beaming. "What's going on?"

"It's a . . . it's a . . ." stuttered Emily.

"It's a midnight feast," snapped Lulu.

"Yummy!" said Olaf, sitting down at the kitchen table. "Can I join in?"

Lulu watched him in horror. There, right in front of him, was the baby's bottle with milk in for Tufty. She'd left it there when she went out in the garden to search for the strange light.

Olaf picked it up. "What's this?"

The princesses exchanged looks.

"It's mine!" said Lulu defiantly. "I still like to drink milk like that." And to prove it, she grabbed the baby's bottle and took a huge slurp.

"Really? From a baby's bottle?" said Olaf, looking puzzled.

"That's right," said Lulu, taking another drink. The bottle made a glugging sound. Emily gave a snort and turned away to hide her giggles.

With Olaf waiting expectantly for the midnight feast to begin, the girls began to look for some food. Clarabel found a jelly and spooned it into dishes and Lulu added some chocolate. They gulped theirs down and then watched impatiently as Olaf ate his incredibly slowly.

Suddenly, footsteps sounded in the corridor. The princesses froze, listening as the steps came closer. They exchanged worried looks, but it was too late to clear everything away. The door swung open and Lady Malika walked into the room. "Princesses!" She raised her dark eyebrows in surprise. "What's going on, and why are you all dressed?"

"We're having a midnight feast," said the princesses, at exactly the same time.

Lady Malika's eyebrows rose even higher. "Is everything all right, Lulu? I thought I heard a strange noise coming from your room, a sort of scratching sound. Is there something in there?"

"Oh, it's probably just a lizard walking

on the roof," said Lulu quickly. "We should go upstairs and get some sleep now."

"Yes, I think you should," replied Lady Malika. "And you as well, Prince Olaf."

The girls trooped upstairs, said goodnight and closed their doors. Lulu waited until she'd heard Olaf's bedroom door click shut and her aunt's door close, too. Then she opened hers a tiny crack. Emily, Clarabel and Jaminta were peeking out of their rooms as well. Quietly, with their very best ninja steps, they prowled downstairs and out into the garden.

"I just hope this works on that lock," murmured Jaminta, tucking the fork she'd borrowed into her pocket.

Reaching the garden shed in seconds, the princesses crouched down next to the door in the ground. The rectangle of wood was easy to see now that its covering of earth was swept to one side. Jaminta wiggled one prong of the fork inside the lock. She twisted and jiggled, until finally there was a low clunk.

"I think I've done it," she said. "Let's try the handle again."

Lulu and Emily grabbed the handle together and yanked it towards them. The rectangle of wood swung upwards with an enormous creak. A hole opened up in front of them, with broad stone steps stretching downwards into darkness.

"Where do you think it leads to?" asked Clarabel.

"There's only one way to find out," replied Lulu, climbing down the steps. "But we have to be really quiet, in case a lion is loose down here."

Clarabel gulped, then she and Emily followed Lulu carefully down the steps.

Jaminta found a wheelbarrow and parked it in front of the hole.

"It won't hide the hole from close up," she explained to the others, "but at least it'll stop anyone seeing it from a distance. I don't want to pull the door shut in case we can't open it from the inside."

"Good idea," said Clarabel, shuddering at the thought of being trapped underground.

"We should have brought torches," Lulu called back.

"I've brought my light bracelet. You take it, Lulu." Jaminta drew an emerald bracelet from her pocket and passed it forward. The jewels lit up the tunnel with a bright green glow.

"Thanks!" Lulu held the bracelet in front of her and carried on down the stone steps, followed by the others.

It seemed a long way down. But when

the stairs ended, they stood in a narrow tunnel with a floor of reddish earth. The air smelled musty.

They tiptoed through the passageway, finding their way by the light from the bracelet. At first the tunnel sloped downwards, until gradually, it began to slope uphill again. The tunnel wall felt cool beneath Lulu's fingers.

"I wonder how far we've gone," murmured Emily.

"Hold on!" whispered Lulu. "I think I can hear something."

They stopped and listened. A faint sound of mewing drifted down the tunnel.

"It sounds like Tufty when he wants some milk," said Clarabel.

Lulu's heart beat faster. "It must be the missing lion cubs!"

Running silently, the princesses

followed the sound. The tunnel twisted and turned, and the mewing grew louder.

At last, Lulu stopped at a bend and held up her hand to signal the others to wait. Breathing fast, she peered round the corner. Half of her wanted to find the missing cubs quickly and hug them all tight. The other half of her knew that if the lioness was nearby then they were all in danger. Terrible danger.

Chapter Eleven

The Hollow Mountain

At first, Lulu couldn't see anything except darkness. Determined to be brave, she lifted up the bracelet and cast emerald light round the corner. Ahead of her stretched a cavern so vast that she couldn't see across to the other side. The light from the jewels only just reached the high ceiling.

Something moved on one side of the cavern and her heart missed a beat. "Oh no!" she cried. "The poor cubs!"

"What's wrong?" said the others, crowding behind her.

A small metal cage stood on the earth floor, with the lioness and four cubs trapped inside it. The cubs moved restlessly, tumbling over each other and mewing. The lioness lay still, her eyes staring into the darkness.

Lulu ran towards the cage. But as she got close the lioness stiffened, then sprang up and snarled. Lulu stopped and backed away a little.

"She doesn't know we're trying to help her," said Clarabel.

Lulu's eyes flashed. "Whoever did this doesn't care about animals at all! How could they put wild lions into a tiny cage like that?"

"The poor cubs look so unhappy," said Clarabel, her blue eyes sad.

Lulu walked carefully round the cage

until she found the side with the door.

"Stop, Lulu!" cried Emily. "The lioness could hurt us if we let them out. We need to find another way to do this!"

Lulu put her hands on her hips. She knew Emily was right. Walter had talked to her about safety many times.

"Look at this!" said Jaminta suddenly, touching the wall and gazing at her hand. Her fingers were covered with sparkling crystals.

"I know where we are!" gasped Lulu. "We're inside Shimmer Rock. The stories about the mountain being hollow must be true."

The princesses gazed around them. Instead of reddish earth, the walls of the cavern were studded with millions of little crystals, just like the ones that shimmered when moonlight struck the mountain.

"There are more cages over here."

Jaminta took the emerald bracelet from Lulu and shone it all around the cavern, revealing more metal cages, all standing empty. "And here's another tunnel. I bet it leads out to the grasslands. That's how someone brought the animals in here."

Lulu looked at the metal bars of the lion's cage. "We need to find a way of letting the lions out which still gives us time to get away."

"I know something that might work," said Emily, shaking back her red hair. "Remember how looking at the purple amethyst gem made us feel sleepy? We could see if it has the same effect on the lions."

"Do you think that will really work?" asked Clarabel.

"Maybe," said Jaminta thoughtfully. "And if they fall asleep, we can open the door safely. When they wake up again they can leave the cage by themselves."

"That's a great idea!" cried Lulu, making the lioness growl again. "Then they'll find their way to the tunnel that leads to the grasslands. Lions have a really good sense of smell."

"Lulu and I can fetch the jewel," said Jaminta.

"We'll hide here and keep watch in case the lion stealers come back," said Emily, and Clarabel nodded in agreement.

Lulu and Jaminta ran from the cavern, their feet thudding through the black tunnel. They'd left the emerald bracelet with Emily and Clarabel, so they kept a hand on the wall of the passageway to steady themselves. Dashing up the steps, they climbed out of the hole and ran across the garden. The full moon hung above the palace and the call of a leopard drifted over from the grasslands.

Upstairs, they began searching for the amethyst in Jaminta's bedroom.

"I'm sure I put it in here," whispered Jaminta, opening a drawer and pulling out a small velvet bag.

Lulu held out her hand and Jaminta dropped the amethyst into it. Turning it over in her fingers, Lulu noticed its hexagonal shape and its heart of deepest purple. She gave an enormous yawn, covering her mouth with her hand.

"The jewel works really fast," she muttered to Jaminta, quickly putting it back in the velvet bag before she became any sleepier.

They rushed out of Jaminta's room towards the stairs, when Lulu noticed her own bedroom door standing wide open. Her stomach turned over. The door should be shut. She knew she'd closed it so that Tufty didn't get loose.

"Oh no, where's Tufty?" she hissed, running inside. "Tufty! Where are you?" Her eyes flicked worriedly around the room.

"Maybe he's hiding," said Jaminta, looking behind a cupboard.

Lulu pulled back her bed sheets, searching in her bed and then underneath it. Then she searched her wardrobe, her drawers and everywhere else she could think of.

Tufty was nowhere.

"I can't believe it. He's disappeared." With tears pricking the back of her eyes, Lulu sank down on to her bed. Tufty could be lost in the palace or maybe someone took him away. Where would she go to start looking for him?

The creak of a floorboard made her turn round. Olaf was standing in the doorway.

Lulu leapt up. "Did you come in here tonight? Did you leave my door open?" she said fiercely.

Olaf's spiky hair looked silvery in the moonlight. "It wasn't me, but I did see somebody come in here. I watched them through a crack in my door. But it was too dark to see who it was." He pushed up his baggy pyjama sleeves.

"Did you hear anything strange?" asked Jaminta.

"There was a noise that sounded like an animal," said Olaf.

"Tufty!" said Lulu sadly. "He's a lion cub who's lost his family."

Olaf chuckled. "Were you looking after him? I thought that you princesses were up to something! I guess that's what the baby bottle was for, then?"

Lulu nodded, a hollow feeling growing inside her. She missed Tufty already.

"Well, you can't give up on him now," said Olaf. "Here, take my torch and this chocolate. When the kings and queens wake up, I'll tell them that you and your friends have gone for an early drive across the grasslands. That'll give you lots of time to find him."

Lulu stared at him. "You'd cover for us? After the way I've been really grumpy towards you?"

"It would be my pleasure!" said Olaf, and swept her a bow.

Lulu bit her lip to stop a smile. He looked so funny bowing in those baggy pyjamas. But underneath she felt awful about how she'd treated him. He'd seemed annoying, but now she could see he was actually very kind.

"Thank you, Olaf," said Jaminta, taking the torch.

Lulu put the chocolate bar in her pocket

and patted Olaf on the shoulder. "I'm really sorry I've been so snappy to you. When all this is over, you can use my gymnastics equipment as much as you like!"

Olaf smiled and bowed again. "Good luck, princesses!"

Chapter Twelve

The Sleep Jewel

Lulu and Jaminta crept back out into the courtyard, pausing by the fountain.

"The person who's stolen Tufty must be the same person who's captured the other lions," cried Lulu. "They could be driving away with him right now!"

"I know," said Jaminta. "But I think we should take the amethyst gem to Emily and Clarabel, and tell them what's going on."

They climbed down into the hole and

switched on Olaf's torch. Going down the steps and along the passageway would be much easier now that they had a light. They sprinted down the tunnel, the torchlight bouncing as they ran. Turning the corner, they stopped inside the vast cavern with its walls of glittering crystals. Emily and Clarabel hurried over to meet them.

"Did you find the amethyst?" asked Clarabel.

Lulu held it out to show them, as she tried to catch her breath. "Don't look at it for too long," she warned them. "It makes you sleepy really fast."

"We've explored the cavern and found another way out," Emily told her. "There's a wider tunnel which leads to the foot of the mountain."

"We're sure that the lioness will catch the scent of the grasslands and escape that way," added Clarabel.

"Great! And when we've released these lions, we have to go and look for Tufty," said Lulu, and she explained how Olaf had seen someone take the little cub from her room.

"Poor Tufty! There's no time to lose!" said Emily. "Let's see if the amethyst works."

Lulu crept towards the lion's cage with the amethyst hidden in the palm of her hand. The little cubs took no notice of her. But as she came closer, the lioness began a long, low growl. Crouching down slowly, Lulu laid the amethyst next to the bars of the cage. The lioness stared at it and the cubs bounced over to look, spellbound by its sparkling purple shape.

Stealing back to the others, Lulu made them turn away from the jewel.

"If we're not careful, we'll end up

gazing at it," she hissed. "Then we'll
fall asleep too." She nudged Clarabel,
who was taking a sideways peep at the
amethyst.

The minutes seemed endless as they
waited. But finally, when the cave felt
very still and quiet, Lulu dared to peek
round.

"It's worked!" she whispered.

All the lions were still, their furry
golden bodies stretched out peacefully.
Even the lioness had laid her head on the
earth, her eyes shut tight.

Clarabel smiled. "The cubs look even
cuter when they're sleeping."

"We must be quick," said Jaminta. "We
don't know how long they'll sleep for."

Lulu strode up to the cage door. But
just as she was about to open it, footsteps
came from the other end of the cave. She
shone Olaf's torch towards the sound and

a figure emerged from a tunnel, carrying a bundle.

Lulu's mouth dropped open. It was the tall figure and long black dress of Lady Malika.

When she saw the girls, Lady Malika stopped, her face twisting furiously.

"I don't believe it!" whispered Emily.

But Lulu couldn't speak. How could the thief be her aunt? It didn't make sense. Then she remembered how her aunt had wanted the princesses to come and stay, so that she would keep away from the grasslands. Her aunty had been awake last night too and could easily have taken Tufty.

"What are you nosy girls doing here?" snapped Lady Malika, her voice echoing round the cavern. "These are my beasts! I captured them and brought them here in my truck, ready to be put to work in the circus. I won't have you meddlesome princesses getting in my way!"

Lulu recovered her voice. "You're not taking them anywhere, and we'll tell the king and queen unless you leave right now!"

"Dreadful princesses!" screeched Lady Malika. Then she dropped her bundle on the floor, turned on her heels and fled back into the shadows.

Lulu breathed in sharply. Was the bundle what she hoped it would be? She raced across the cavern. Scooping it up, she kissed the furry ears and wriggly body of a little lion cub.

"Tufty! It's really you!" She beamed at him in delight.

Inside the cage, the lioness rolled over with a grunt but didn't open her eyes.

"Quickly, Lulu!" whispered Jaminta. Holding Tufty under one arm, Lulu

undid the catch of the cage and pulled.
But the door didn't budge.

"There's a second catch, really high
up," said Emily, pointing at it.

Lulu put Tufty into Clarabel's arms
and stretched up to reach the other door
catch. "I – can't – get – to – it!" she said
between clenched teeth.

Looking around, she noticed a piece of
rock jutting out of the wall near the cage.
She scrambled up on to it and looked
down on the metal bars below her.

"Wait, Lulu! You aren't going to jump,
are you?" called Clarabel.

"I have to," replied Lulu, and keeping
her eyes on the metal roof, she made an
enormous leap off the rock to land on the
top of the cage with a bang. The lioness
below her opened her eyes, then shut
them again.

Holding her breath, Lulu crawled to

the edge of the bars, stretched over and flicked open the catch. Then she stood up, back-flipped off the roof and landed gracefully on the ground.

Jaminta swung the cage door open. Clarabel handed Tufty back to Lulu, who kissed him one more time and placed him gently in the cage. He scampered up to his brothers and sisters and lay down next to them with a happy mew. Lulu left the cage door open and backed away.

"Ready?" asked Jaminta, preparing to grab the amethyst.

Lulu looked at Tufty. She didn't want to leave him, but she knew she had to give him this chance to be a wild cub once again. "Yes, ready!" she said.

Jaminta grabbed the purple gem and they tiptoed out of the cavern. They crept round the corner into the narrow tunnel and broke into a run. Clarabel stumbled over a loose rock, but Lulu helped her up. Sprinting hard, they didn't stop until they reached the bottom of the stone steps that led to the palace garden. A square of yellow light at the top told them that the sun would soon be rising.

The princesses paused, trying to catch their breath.

A deafening roar swept down the tunnel, making the floor and walls tremble.

"The lioness!" cried Lulu. "She's woken up."

They climbed as fast as they could and scrambled out of the hole at the top. Then together they heaved the old wooden door shut and pushed a wheelbarrow right on top of it, just to be sure that nothing could get out that way.

"We did it!" Emily bounced up and down. "We freed all the lions!"

"And Tufty got his family back again," said Lulu.

As Jaminta tucked the amethyst sleep jewel away in her pocket, Clarabel noticed something else in her hand. "What's that you're holding, Jaminta?" she asked.

Jaminta held out one hand to show them dozens of sparkling stones. "I picked up some crystals inside the cave. I'm going to try making powerful jewels with them. If the Onica Heart Crystals were made from stones like these, they must be really special."

A golden sun peeped over the horizon, sending a warm glow across the palace garden. The princesses sat down on the ground, their legs aching.

Lulu fumbled in her pocket and pulled out the chocolate that Olaf had given her. She broke off big pieces and handed them round. The chocolate tasted especially sweet after all that running down the tunnel.

"What a strange mystery that was," said Emily. "The lions were hidden under the mountain all this time."

"Not any more." Lulu smiled, her eyes sparkling. "I bet they're already heading back to the grasslands where they belong."

Chapter Thirteen

A Royal Circus Show

The princesses stumbled, yawning, into breakfast that morning. They'd changed out of their dusty clothes into long silk dresses and their favourite tiaras, hoping that the kings and queens wouldn't notice anything different.

Lulu shook back her wavy black hair as she sat down at the table. She felt so sleepy, but a large helping of pancakes and syrup began to make her feel better.

"I hope the deportment lessons aren't

tiring you out, Lulu," said Queen Shani, looking at the dark circles under her daughter's eyes.

Lulu glanced at the other princesses and bit her lip to hide a smile. "Not really. But maybe I should have a rest from them for a little while."

"Just for a little while." The queen nodded and turned to her husband. "I'm just so disappointed with Lady Malika."

"Yes, dear," replied the king, passing her the teapot. "I'm glad she was caught."

"Huh? What's that?" Lulu's lion-like eyes flashed at the mention of her aunt.

"Please speak gently, my dear," said the queen. "We received a message from Walter this morning. He found several wild animals from the grasslands in Lady Malika's circus, mainly zebras and leopards. She must have taken them from here by truck. Thankfully, those animals are back in the wild now and the circus has been closed."

The princesses exchanged looks. Lady Malika had wanted the lions to perform in her circus too. At least now she couldn't hurt animals any more.

"I think circuses should just have human performers," said Olaf loudly. "I'd love to show you the circus skills I've been practising."

Lulu beamed at him. For a prince, Olaf was really good fun. "Why don't we do circus skills together? All five of us," she said. "We'll practise this morning and put on a show after lunch."

"I'll juggle!" cried Emily.

"I'll walk on stilts," added Jaminta.

Clarabel frowned for a moment, then smiled mysteriously.

❤

So, after lunch, the table was moved from the Great Hall and the kings and queens of Undala and Finia, and Lulu's deportment teacher, Madame Rez, sat down to watch the circus show.

First of all, Olaf walked along the balance beam. Then Lulu followed with a series of tumbles across the floor, ending with a back flip. Emily and Jaminta managed good displays of juggling and stilt-walking. Then a funny figure with a red nose and enormous checked trousers wobbled in, and started falling over and making the audience burst out laughing.

Lulu grinned to see Clarabel performing so well as a clown. When the clown act had ended, Lulu finished off the show by walking on her hands in front of the audience while balancing a book on her feet.

"Bravo!" cried Madame Rez.

"Magnificent show, Lulu! You can balance the book on your feet in our next lesson."

When all the clapping had died down, Queen Shani rose from her seat. "Well done, all of you! Lulu, we're very proud of your acrobatic skills, and this seems the perfect time to give this to you." She handed a wrapped parcel to her daughter.

Surprised, Lulu tore open the paper and pulled out a beautiful yellow leotard, decorated with golden star sequins. The princesses gathered round to admire it.

"Now you can practise your acrobatics looking like a proper gymnast," explained the king.

"It's fantastic! Thank you," said Lulu, giving her parents a hug.

💜

The princesses and Olaf watched the sun

set on the grasslands that evening. Ally drove them up to the hollow to see the lioness and her cubs in their grasslands home once more. A herd of elephants wandered past, kicking up the reddish earth, and in the distance giraffes were eating from the trees. The princesses watched the lion cubs fondly.

"I'm so glad they found their way back," said Clarabel.

"And they look so happy," added Emily.

Lulu smiled as Tufty chased his brothers and sisters round and round. He stopped and gazed at her for a moment with his big brown eyes. Then he carried on scampering through the bushes.

"Where's the lioness? I wish I could see her as well," said Olaf.

"She's probably lying down," said Lulu. "Climb up the tree and you'll get a good view from there."

The princesses had to help him up a little. But after some shoving, Olaf managed to shin up the tree. "You're right! I've got a great view from up here." His voice was faint as he called down from the very top.

Lulu grinned at her friends. "For a prince, he's really not that bad."

"He's definitely one of the good ones," agreed Jaminta, taking the Shimmer Rock crystals from her pocket for another look.

"Be careful with those stones," said Ally, looking round from the driver's seat. "If you join them together they'll be very valuable and powerful, just like the Onica Heart Crystals."

"Don't worry. We'll be careful," said Jaminta.

"But we like to be adventurous too," said Lulu, swinging herself into the tree and hanging upside down.

"I don't know which is wilder, Lulu. You or the lion cubs," laughed Ally.

"There's nothing wilder than a Rescue Princess!" said Lulu.

The Rescue Princesses
The Stolen Crystals

Paula Harrison

nosy crow

For Mum and Dad, with much love

Chapter One

The Master Gem Maker

Princess Jaminta dashed up the stairs
with her long, green cloak flying out
behind her. She ran into her bedroom,
undid her cloak and threw it on to the
bed. Her brown eyes sparkled.

She'd just been to see the little panda
cub that lived on Cloud Mountain with
his mother. He was such a sweet thing,
with big black eyes and a cuddly white
tummy. She wished she could have stayed
up there all day!

Quickly, she gave herself a shake. She must stop daydreaming about the little cub! She had something important to do.

Hurrying to her dressing table, she picked up a small lump of white rock that lay in front of the mirror. It was time to do something special with this rock crystal.

She had made it by sticking lots of tiny crystals together. It didn't look very pretty yet. But once she had worked on it with her jewel-making tools, it would turn into a beautiful gem which would be perfect for her grandfather's birthday present. She had to hurry, though! His birthday was tomorrow and soon the other royal families from all over the world would be arriving to help them celebrate.

She unfolded her pouch of jewel-making tools and picked up a silver chisel. Her smooth dark hair curled round her chin as she leaned forward. Holding the rock crystal still, she tapped on the chisel with a tiny hammer. She would smooth its sides and change its shape.

Maybe it could be heart-shaped, just like the famous Onica Heart Crystals that used to belong to her grandfather. Those Heart Crystals had vanished long ago, but everyone in the kingdom still talked about them.

She tapped the rock harder. Delicate white flakes chipped off and dropped on to the dressing table. But the crystal still looked rough and absolutely refused to sparkle.

Jaminta frowned. Why was it so difficult? It wasn't as if she'd never done this before. She'd been making jewels for years. She'd even made the special rings that she and the other Rescue Princesses used to call each other when they needed

245

help. She smiled for a moment, thinking of Emily, Clarabel and Lulu. Together they had made a secret promise always to help an animal in trouble. She was so proud that her special jewels played an important part in their animal rescues.

Gripping the chisel hard, she held it against the rock crystal once more and gave three swift taps with the hammer. There was a snap and a jagged crack ran all the way down the side of the rock. Jaminta gasped. She'd tapped too hard. How could she have been so silly?

She should have started making the jewel weeks ago instead of spending all her time with the panda cub. Now it was far too late to make Grandfather a different present. She rubbed her eyes with the back of her hand. The jewel was ruined. Unless . . . maybe . . . she'd nearly forgotten about the one person who could help.

She flung the tools down and fled from the room, taking the lump of rock with her. Swift as a mountain deer, she ran down five flights of stairs. She passed the kitchens, where the clash of saucepans told her that the banquet was cooking.

She passed the great hall, where her mother was piling twelve round tiers of birthday cake on top of each other. In the driveway, she passed the servants hanging red and gold paper lanterns between every tree.

Ignoring all the party preparations, Jaminta hurried down the outside steps and along a winding path. She stopped in front of a wooden hut in the furthest corner of the garden. The sound of clinking metal came from inside and a warm orange light shone from the windows. This was where the Master Gem

Maker worked, and he knew more about crafting jewels than anyone else in the Kingdom of Onica.

Jaminta knocked on the door.

A small man with round spectacles opened the door and bowed. "Good afternoon, Princess Jaminta. Aren't you getting ready for the party? I thought all the royal visitors were arriving today." He stepped aside to let Jaminta through the door.

"They should be here very soon," said Jaminta. "But I was just trying to finish Grandfather's present and then something went wrong." She held out the lump of crystal for him to see. The crack running down one side seemed even bigger than before.

The Master Gem Maker took the rough jewel from her hand and studied it carefully with a magnifying glass.

Jaminta watched him anxiously. Then she swept a quick look round the room. The workshop was crammed with even more jewels and equipment than the last time she had been here. Shelves lined the walls, full of tools and little pots of polish.

A wooden chest stood open on the floor, bursting with every kind of gem. There were ocean-blue sapphires, forest-green emeralds and rubies as red as fire. They dazzled her eyes and sent sparkles of coloured light dancing across the wooden ceiling. She remembered how she used to come here every day when she was little, to learn jewel crafting from the Master.

"What kind of gem are you trying to make?" asked the Master Gem Maker.

"I wanted to make it heart-shaped because it's for Grandfather's birthday," Jaminta said miserably. "He always says that the kingdom hasn't been the same since the Onica Heart Crystals were stolen. I thought if I made him a crystal that looked the same, he'd be pleased."

"It's nearly ten years since the Heart Crystals were stolen," said the Master. "Each one was as clear as a diamond with a flickering flame right in the centre. Those jewels were so magical that they could reveal the true nature of a person's heart."

A gust of wind from the mountains swept round the hut, sending an icy chill under the door and making the windows rattle.

Jaminta bit her lip. "I collected lots of tiny crystals at a place called Shimmer Rock and stuck them all together. I thought it would be beautiful."

The Master placed the rock crystal back into Jaminta's hand and looked at her over the top of his spectacles. "You can

251

still make something special. You just
need to do one more thing."

Jaminta felt her heart leap. "What is it?
What do I have to do?"

"You must dip it into the Silver River."

Jaminta stared at him, open mouthed.
"Really? I just have to put it in the river?"

The Master Gem Maker smiled. "The
river has a natural magic. You can't
use it to turn a frog into a prince or a
pumpkin into a carriage, but you can
change a crystal to its true shape. Go
there at sunrise. That's when the magic is
strongest."

"I'll go first thing tomorrow." Jaminta's
face glowed. She could just imagine how
beautiful the jewel was going to look and
how happy her grandfather would be
when she gave it to him.

The Master smiled. "Remember! Only
tell people that you really trust about

your crystal. They're very precious things!"

"I'll remember," said Jaminta. "Thank you!" She hid the rock in her pocket and opened the door, then turned back for a moment. "If only I could find the lost Heart Crystals for Grandfather as well!"

The Master Gem Maker's eyes turned hazy, as if he was gazing at something far away. "Crystals are full of surprises. Maybe one day the Heart Crystals will return."

Jaminta was about to ask him what he meant, but just then the deep clear sound of a bell rang out from the palace.

Jaminta caught her breath. That was the signal. The royal visitors were arriving. Soon she would see the other Rescue Princesses again!

Chapter Two

Emperor Cho's Ninetieth Birthday

Jaminta raced back towards the palace, a fizzing feeling growing inside her. She could hardly believe that the river was magical, although she'd always thought it was special somehow. Now she knew exactly how to turn her rock crystal into a proper jewel ready for Grandfather's birthday.

Her grandfather was Emperor Cho, the ruler of the Kingdom of Onica, and tomorrow he would be ninety years old.

There would be games, feasting and fireworks. Jaminta could hardly wait! More than anything, she longed to show the Rescue Princesses her beautiful panda cub. She knew they would love him as much as she did.

The bell rang out again from the top of the high pagoda roof.

Jaminta scanned the driveway, but there was no sign of the visitors yet. She ran up the palace steps and gazed at the purple mountain peaks soaring beyond the river. Thick, green bamboo forests stretched halfway up the slopes, leaving bare rock at the very top. The cold breeze from the mountains tickled her cheeks. It wasn't winter yet, but soon the peaks would be covered in snow.

She swung round as her grandfather came out of the palace door behind her.

"There you are, Jaminta!" Emperor

Cho climbed slowly down the steps. His grey hair looked thin, but his brown eyes twinkled at her.

Jaminta smiled back, secretly checking that her rock crystal was hidden deep inside her pocket. Tomorrow at sunrise she would take it down to the river, just like the Master Gem Maker had told her.

"Are the visitors nearly here, Grandfather?" she asked.

"Yes. Look, you can see the carriages." The emperor pointed at the road that led up from the valley.

Jaminta spotted the long caterpillar of carriages trundling up the hill. As they moved closer, she could see kings, queens, princes and princesses waving from the carriage windows. Her eyes searched for three princesses, one with black hair, one with golden hair and one with wild red curls.

Soon the carriages climbed the hill to the palace gate and passed between stone pillars with statues of dragons on top. They drew to a stop. Princess Emily appeared, climbing out of the first carriage, her red curls waving in the breeze.

"Emily!" Jaminta hugged her friend. "I'm so happy you could come!"

"Hello, Jaminta!" said Emily, hugging her back.

Emily's parents, the King and Queen of Middingland, climbed out next. Then Emily's maid, Ally, appeared carrying Emily's pink suitcase. She smiled at Jaminta, who grinned back. Ally had once been an undercover agent who caught jewel thieves. She had used ninja skills when she was an agent and had taught them to the princesses to help with their animal rescues.

"Your Majesties!" Emperor Cho bowed to the King and Queen of Middingland. "Thank you for coming all this way to celebrate my birthday!"

Suddenly, another figure hopped out of the Middingland carriage. She looked just like Emily, except that her red hair was even curlier and her eyes were a sparkling green.

"Hurry *up*, Lottie. You're being so slow." Emily turned to Jaminta. "This is my little sister, Lottie. She didn't come along last time the royal families gathered together because she was staying with our cousins."

"Hello, Lottie." Jaminta smiled.

Lottie stuck out her tongue and then grinned cheekily.

The next carriage drew to a halt, and a tall man with a red cloak and a crooked mouth clambered out, followed by his

259

servant.

"Welcome back to Onica, Earl Scrant," said the emperor. "I don't think we've met for many years."

"Greetings." Earl Scrant bowed stiffly before walking away. Unluckily, he bumped straight into Ally and sent the pink suitcase flying. He glared at her and then marched on, his red cloak billowing out around him.

"Sorry, sir. Please excuse me," said Ally, darting a mysterious look at the earl.

Jaminta noticed Ally's strange glance as she ran over to help pick up the suitcase.

One by one, Emperor Cho greeted all the other royal guests. Jaminta's mum and dad, the King and Queen of Onica, came to greet the visitors too. The orchestra played a beautiful tune and trays of honey cakes were brought around for everyone.

Emperor Cho clapped his hands. "Ladies and gentlemen, kings and queens," he announced. "Welcome to the Kingdom of Onica. There will be feasting, fireworks and a twelve tier birthday cake! This has always been a land of adventures and we hope you enjoy your stay very much!"

A buzz of excitement came from a group of princes standing nearby. "Adventures!" cried Prince George. "I want something really exciting to happen!"

"Poor princes!" said a voice behind Jaminta's ear. "They'll never have the best adventures with us around!"

Jaminta spun round to find Princess Lulu, with her black curls and flashing eyes, standing behind her, grinning. Next to her, stood a smiling Princess Clarabel, tucking her golden hair behind her ear.

"Lulu! Clarabel!" cried Jaminta,

hugging them both. "I'm so glad you're here! I've got something really special I want to show you." She beckoned her three friends to follow her to the palace gate. She would take them straight up to Cloud Mountain to see the panda cub and tell them her big secret about Grandfather's birthday present and the magical river on the way.

"Jaminta! Princesses! Come back please!" the Queen of Onica called after them. "You must all come with me and choose a fan ready for the banquet tonight. It's an important custom here in the Kingdom of Onica for ladies to carry fans, you know! And it will make you look graceful and elegant." She began to shepherd the princesses towards the palace door.

Jaminta groaned. She wished her mum hadn't noticed them sneaking away.

"Don't worry!" whispered Clarabel, squeezing her hand. "Maybe this won't take long."

"Come along, princesses!" said the queen. "You're very lucky girls to be borrowing Onican fans. Put your best dresses on and then join me in the Fan Room." She waved her hand majestically to send them hurrying away.

Jaminta clomped up the stairs, frowning. Who wanted to spend time looking at fans when there was a cute panda cub to play with?

Chapter Three

Fan-tastic
Princesses

Jaminta showed her friends to their
rooms then trudged crossly to her own.
She pulled her new dress out of her
wardrobe. It had been sewn especially
for the emperor's birthday celebrations
and was made of shimmering green silk
decorated with gold blossoms. It had
wide sleeves that hung elegantly below
her arms. She pulled it over her head and
dropped the rock crystal that she'd taken
to the Master Gem Maker into her pocket.

Then she added a gold tiara and with one last look in the mirror, she made her way to the Fan Room.

The other princesses arrived in their best dresses, too. Emily was wearing a pink dress with a wide skirt, while Clarabel's dress was very long in a beautiful pale blue. Lulu, who was gazing longingly out of the window at the mountains, wore a shorter yellow dress decorated with beads.

"Ready, girls?" said the queen. "Let me show you our fan collection." She opened a large display case filled with beautiful fans in every colour. Many of them shone with sequins or tiny pearls. Jaminta chose one which had been painted with a picture of the Silver River and the mountains beyond.

When all the princesses had finished choosing, the queen closed the case

again. "Now I'll show you how to use them. Place your thumb behind the fan, like this." She twisted the fan, showing them what she meant. "Then you must make the fan flutter quickly and delicately, like this."

The princesses copied her, trying hard to use the fan just as elegantly. Lulu flapped hers a bit too hard and knocked off Jaminta's tiara, sending them both into fits of giggles.

A maid appeared in the doorway and curtsied. "Excuse me, Your Majesty. The Chief Cook would like to speak to you about the noodles."

"Carry on practising, girls," said the queen, as she hurried away. "And remember, the banquet starts at six o' clock. Don't be late!"

"Yes, Your Majesty," they all said, with a curtsy.

"I think these fans are lovely," said Clarabel, wafting hers, which was decorated with pearls and soft blue feathers.

Lulu groaned. "They're nice, but I want to stop waving them now. I mean, what good are they?"

"I know!" said Emily suddenly, her hazel eyes sparkling. "They could be really handy for our ninja moves!"

"Really?" said Lulu. "How would you use a fan for ninja moves?"

Emily flipped her fan open in front of her face, disappearing behind its red and gold pattern. "See? You can hide behind them!"

"You can do more than that," said Jaminta. "I've been using them since I was little. Watch this!" And she flicked her wrist, sending her fan across the room in a graceful arc. It swept over the top of a fruit bowl, knocking into a bunch of oranges, which rolled away across the floor. The fan landed on the windowsill and closed with a neat snap.

"Awesome!" said Lulu. "You have to teach us how to do that!"

"Are you sure we're allowed?" asked Clarabel, her blue eyes wide.

"Don't worry! The fans are too strong to get damaged," said Jaminta. "It's quite easy. I'll show you!" She fetched her fan and flicked it again, making it land in exactly the same place on the window sill.

The other princesses had a go next, and soon there was a flurry of whizzing fans and falling oranges.

"I'll tell Ally about this," said Emily. "Maybe she knows some ninja moves using fans as well."

When the fruit bowl was empty, the

princesses hurried to gather up the fallen oranges. Some had rolled away under a long table, so they crawled underneath it to collect them. They were just about to crawl out again, when they heard voices and heavy footsteps.

Jaminta pulled the others back under the table and yanked the tablecloth down to hide them. "If we climb out now, we'll get told off for not being all prim and proper!" she hissed. "Let's stay under here till they've gone."

The voices grew louder. Jaminta peered out from under the fringe of the tablecloth and saw two pairs of men's shoes walk across the room and stop next to the window. The first shoes were black and had been polished until they shone. The other shoes were brown and scuffed.

Jaminta thought she caught a glimpse of red material as they passed by. But she couldn't see much more without sticking her head right out into the open.

"Hurry up!" said a man in a thin, bossy voice. "I have something important to say and I don't want everyone hearing it."

Jaminta's heart raced. What was it that this man didn't want other people to hear?

"We're going up the mountain, to look for those lost things," said the thin voice. "Make sure you bring your shovel with you."

"What things, Your Grace?" said a second man, sounding confused.

"Wake up!" snapped the thin voice. "The special things I left here ten years ago. You know what I'm talking about."

"But, Your Grace! We searched for them several times. You said they were lost."

"We couldn't look for them properly back then because we were being followed," said the thin voice, rising in annoyance. "But this is a perfect opportunity. It's not often I get to come back to Onica without everyone getting suspicious. Once I've found a likely place, you will begin digging."

A hand closed around Jaminta's wrist. It was Emily. She pointed at the polished black shoes and pulled a face.

Jaminta wasn't sure what she meant and didn't dare ask out loud. Her mind was whirling. What were the men looking for on the mountainside? And why was it so secret?

Chapter Four

Gem Song

The princesses tried to keep completely still under the table as the men carried on talking.

"But what if the sun goes down while I'm there on the mountainside?" said the second man. "They say great black and white bears roam the forest."

"They're pandas, you brainless fool! They won't hurt you," said the thin voice. "Now, meet me by the bridge in two hours and don't forget your shovel."

"Yes, My Lord," came the low reply, and the scuffed brown shoes marched away.

The black shoes stayed by the window for a few minutes, then they left too. The princesses crawled out, carefully checking that the room was empty.

"Phew!" said Clarabel. "I thought they were never going to leave."

"I've met one of them before," said Emily. "That's what I was trying to tell you. I recognised the voice of the bossy one, the one in the black shoes."

"Is he from Middingland?" asked Lulu.

Emily screwed up her face, thinking hard. "Yes, that must be how I know him. I just can't remember his name."

Jaminta put the oranges back in the bowl and picked up her fan. "I wonder what they're looking for. I've never heard of anything being lost on the mountain. I hope they don't disturb the animals when they go up there."

"Are there really pandas in the forest?" asked Clarabel.

"Yes there are!" said Jaminta. "We could sneak away and see them, now that my mum's gone to the kitchens." She grinned. "And guess what? One of the pandas is a baby!"

"A baby panda! How lovely!" cried Clarabel, her blue eyes sparkling.

"I've never seen a panda in real life before!" said Emily. "Is the cub really sweet?"

Jaminta nodded. "He's gorgeous!"

Not wanting to wait another second, the princesses put their fans away in a drawer and raced downstairs. People were still unloading suitcases from the carriages and carrying them inside.

Jaminta led them through the gardens. They passed trees with crimson leaves and a pond full of golden fish. At last they reached the back gate to the palace grounds.

Jaminta unfastened the gate. The princesses burst through and raced down the rough grassy slope. They stopped to catch their breath at the bottom, where a fast-moving river flowed along the valley.

"Oh! I nearly forgot! I've got something else to show you, too." Jaminta pulled her rock crystal out of her pocket and showed it to them.

The other princesses stared at the lump of rock with its rough edges and dirty-white surface.

"Er . . . what is it?" said Lulu.

"It's a rock crystal," said Jaminta. "I've found out the secret of how to change its shape. When I've turned it into a beautiful jewel, I'm going to give it to my grandfather for his birthday."

"So what's the secret? How do you change it?" said Emily.

"I have to put it in the river at sunrise," Jaminta smiled. "The river will change it, because it's magical."

The princesses stared at the river. It really did look magical with the sunshine dancing on its surface.

"Wow! That's amazing!" said Clarabel. "We'll come with you tomorrow morning to help."

Jaminta smiled gratefully at Clarabel, then Lulu burst out: "That's great, but can we get going now? I'm dying to see the baby panda!"

Jaminta sighed and put the rock back into her pocket. Maybe when the crystal had changed into something beautiful, Lulu would be more interested in it. She wished she could make it happen right now, but the Master Gem Maker had told her that the magic was strongest at sunrise.

The girls walked along to the curved red bridge which arched across the river. Their feet drummed on the wooden planks as they crossed and the river bubbled over the stones below them. On the other side, the ground sloped steeply upwards. They soon found themselves inside a thick forest where bamboo trees stretched straight up to the sky. Now and then they caught a glimpse of the palace below, which became smaller and smaller as they climbed higher up Cloud Mountain.

"I hope those men from the Fan Room aren't around here," said Clarabel, nervously.

"Don't worry," said Jaminta. "It's a very big forest so I'm sure we won't see them."

They pushed their way through the

closely growing trees until they reached the edge of a rocky ravine. A narrow rope bridge spanned the steep drop.

"It's best if we go one at a time," Jaminta told them. "The bridge isn't very strong."

One by one, the princesses crossed the swaying rope bridge, trying not to look at the rocks below them. Even Jaminta, who was used to the wobbly bridge, was glad to be safely on the other side.

"There's a clearing up here," she said. "That's where I often see the pandas."

Listening hard, the girls crept towards a gap in the trees. The sound of cracking and rustling came from up ahead. Jaminta smiled. That would be the mother panda, pulling down bamboo to feed herself and her baby.

A sudden tug on her pocket made her check the rock crystal. It felt heavier somehow. Maybe she was just tired from all the climbing. It couldn't really be heavier than it was before.

Together, they tiptoed into the clearing and looked around. They were quite high up the slope now. Mist had rolled down from the mountain peaks and it hung over the grass like a magic spell. On the far side next to a rocky outcrop sat two furry black and white shapes. One big and one small.

Clarabel gasped. "Look! There's the little cub with his mother!"

"The cub is so cute!" said Emily, admiringly.

"He's lovely, isn't he!" agreed Jaminta. The panda cub looked up at the sound of her voice, his ears twitching. "I come up here to see him all the time. Now that he's older he loves to climb and play. Sometimes his mother leaves him here

while she goes to gather more food."

"Have you given him a name?" asked Lulu.

"No, I haven't," said Jaminta. "Maybe we can think of one together."

The mother panda swung round, looking in the direction of their voices. Then she went back to chomping long stems of bamboo again.

"I think they've got used to me," added Jaminta. "They don't seem to mind me being here at all."

The mother panda ambled away into the forest and the sound of shaking bamboo trees came from her direction.

The princesses watched the little cub bound back and forth underneath the rocky outcrop. Then he climbed up a tree, pulling at the trunk with his little paws. Halfway up, he lost his grip and slid back down, landing on the earth on his furry white bottom.

The princesses giggled.

The cub gave up on the tree trunk and started trying to climb up the rocky outcrop instead. Higher and higher he went, until only his little black legs could be seen below the rock jutting out of the hillside.

The princesses crept closer to watch him, and a sudden weight in her pocket made Jaminta check her rock crystal again. Why did it feel so strange and heavy? She glanced at the other princesses, but they hadn't noticed her worried look.

"I didn't know pandas could climb like that," said Emily.

Just then a noise rang out across the clearing. It was a lovely sound, so high and sweet that for a moment Jaminta thought one of her friends had started singing.

She looked all around the clearing. "What *is* that sound?"

But the other princesses were staring straight at her.

"It's you, Jaminta!" said Lulu. "It's coming from your pocket."

The sound grew louder and even sweeter, rolling around the clearing and into the forest. Feeling like she was dreaming, Jaminta reached into her pocket and pulled out the lump of crystal. It shook as her fingers closed round it and she knew that it really was this strange, rough gem making the noise. She lifted it up to the light and the sound changed into a sequence of musical notes that rang out like a chiming bell.

There was a silence after the last note died away.

"That was really strange!" cried Emily.

But before Jaminta could speak, a deep cracking noise broke through the still air. A huge chunk of stone fell off the rocky outcrop and crashed to the ground. A skitter of smaller stones followed and dust rose from the earth below.

The princesses stared in horror at the broken rock.

"Oh no! Where's the cub!" Jaminta cried. "That's where he was climbing!" She started to run towards the rock, her feet flying across the misty grass.

Chapter Five

Being Lucky

"Wait, Jaminta! What about the cub's mother?" called Emily. "Will she mind you going near her baby?"

But Jaminta kept on running, her heart pounding. She'd watched the little panda growing every week since the springtime and she couldn't stand the thought of him being hurt. Skidding to a halt, she scanned the rocky outcrop. There was a jagged slice right across it where the stone had broken away.

A thin cry came from the ground. Jaminta knelt down, holding her breath. The panda cub lay among the fallen rubble. The stones seemed to have missed him, except for a rock which lay across his back paw. He wriggled and gave a frightened mew.

Jaminta reached out and carefully lifted the rock away, setting the little cub free. "There you are. Are you all right now?"

The cub looked up at her, his black eyes solemn.

Amazed at her own daring, Jaminta lifted up the paw that had been trapped and touched it gently. He had soft pads beneath tiny sharp claws, and his fur was so long and soft that it made her want to give him an enormous hug.

"You have to be careful," she told him gently.

The cub yawned, showing rows of little

 287

teeth and a pink tongue.

"Is he all right?" said Clarabel anxiously, as she, Emily and Lulu reached Jaminta's side.

"He was lucky," Jaminta told them. "One paw was trapped but there's no sign of injury."

"That's what we should call him – Lucky!" said Emily. "It really suits him!"

The little panda snuffled at Emily's shoes, as if to show that he liked her idea. "Lucky!" murmured Jaminta. "That *is* a good name for him."

"Let's move these stones and clear a path for him." Lulu began moving the fallen rocks aside.

Emily and Clarabel started to help her.

Jaminta looked round, suddenly remembering the mother panda. But there was no sign of her in the clearing. "Maybe the mother didn't see what

happened," she said. "She must still be getting bamboo."

Lucky watched the princesses with his big eyes. His white belly looked plump and fluffy. Then with a little mew, he rolled on to all fours and walked down the grassy path that the girls had cleared for him. Only the tiniest limp on his back paw gave away that anything had happened.

There was a loud rustling on the edge of the clearing, and the large shape of the mother panda returned through the trees. The princesses backed away quickly as Lucky skipped over to join his mother. The mother nudged him with her nose and they walked away into the bamboo forest together.

Jaminta gave a deep sigh of relief. "He seems just fine now."

Lulu frowned. "He could have been

badly hurt, though. Maybe you shouldn't bring that crystal thing up here again. It's not safe."

Jaminta stared at her. "It wasn't the crystal's fault. I'm sure it wasn't."

"But it did make that really loud singing sound," said Emily. "Sometimes loud noises can cause a rock fall."

"Poor little cub! I'm so glad he's all right," added Clarabel.

Jaminta gazed at the rock crystal in the palm of her hand, her mind whirling. How could they blame the crystal for what happened? She was sure it wasn't a bad jewel. But why had it felt so heavy just before it started to sing? What if they were right and the crystal really had made the rock shatter?

"We're not saying you did it on purpose, Jaminta," said Clarabel. "Please don't be cross."

Jaminta tried to smile. The rock crystal felt light again as she put it back in her pocket.

"I've never heard of a gem making a sound before," said Lulu. "How did you get it to do that?"

"I didn't!" replied Jaminta. "I haven't been able to change its shape at all yet."

"It was such a beautiful song," said Clarabel. "Maybe it means something."

"Maybe," said Jaminta with a frown. "I just wish I knew what it was."

"Come on! Let's go back," said Emily. "It'll be time for the banquet soon."

The mist started to fade as the girls made their way through the forest. They came out of the trees and headed towards the wooden bridge that spanned the river.

"Lucky is so gorgeous," sighed Clarabel. "I wish we had pandas in my kingdom."

Emily nodded. "He has such lovely little paws!"

They climbed on to the wooden bridge and Jaminta heard a noise behind them. She looked back, wondering what it was, and glimpsed a flash of red material disappearing between the trees.

Chapter Six

Spotting a Ninja

When they returned, the princesses found that the banquet was almost ready. Sizzling noises came from the kitchen, along with wonderful cooking smells.

The lump of crystal still felt light inside Jaminta's pocket. She clutched it anxiously. Maybe she should take it to the Master Gem Maker and tell him what had happened in the forest. But the sound of the dinner gong stopped her. There was no time to see him now.

The banquet was about to begin.

The princesses rushed upstairs to brush their hair and straighten their tiaras. Emily wore her favourite tiara, which had beautiful gold leaves woven together. Clarabel's tiara was made from a delicate wiry gold decorated with sapphires and Lulu's was a stunning golden crown. Jaminta checked her own tiara in a nearby mirror. It was shaped into three flowers with white crystals glowing on each petal. It was her only tiara with crystal decorations and it sparkled like the first snow on the mountains.

The dinner gong sounded again and the girls hurried to the Fan Room to collect the fans they'd chosen earlier.

"We'd better not flick the fans at the banquet," said Clarabel.

"I'll try to remember not to!" Lulu's eyes gleamed naughtily.

Smoothing her green silk dress, Jaminta led the princesses back downstairs to join the crowd of kings and queens in the banquet hall. She blinked as she walked into the room. She'd never seen the hall look so amazing. Masses of gold streamers and round red lanterns hung from the ceiling. The princesses gazed at all the delicious food on the tables.

Jaminta pulled out a chair to sit down and stepped on something hard. She gasped. Was that somebody's foot?

"I'm so sorry! I didn't know you were there," she said, looking up to find a tall man with a crooked mouth glaring down at her.

She shivered. He looked so cross that she wondered what he was going to say. But he just turned away, pulling his red cloak around his shoulders. As he marched off, Jaminta suddenly remembered when she'd seen him before. That morning, he had bumped into Ally and knocked over her suitcase. Ally had given him a really strange look and she had wondered why.

"Are you all right?" Clarabel waved her fan next to Jaminta's flushed face.

Jaminta managed a smile. "I'm fine. But I don't think proper princesses are supposed to tread on their guest's toes!"

Emily rushed towards them, nearly knocking a chair over in her hurry. "That's him! That man you just spoke to, Jaminta. He's the one whose voice I recognised. I remember him now!"

"You mean the man who wants to go digging on the mountainside? Are you sure it's him?" said Lulu, looking over Emily's shoulder.

"Completely!" Emily nodded her head knowingly. "He lives in Middingland, where I come from, but he doesn't come to our palace very often." She beckoned them towards her, and when their heads were close together, she whispered, "His name is Earl Scrant."

The princesses all looked at the scowling Earl Scrant, who was now standing on the other side of the room. He was wearing shiny black shoes just like the ones they'd seen from underneath the table.

"We'll have to keep an eye on him," said Lulu firmly. "I don't know what he's digging for, but there's something dodgy about him."

The other princesses nodded.

"What are you all whispering about?" Emily's little sister, Princess Lottie, bounced over to them, her bright eyes inquisitive.

"Nothing! Go back to Mum! The

banquet's about to start," said Emily.

Lottie pouted. "I know you're talking about something secret and *I* want to know what it is!"

"Look! Mum's calling you!" said Emily, hurrying her sister away.

The banquet sped by in a jumble of eating, drinking and talking. The princesses were glad to get away at the end, despite the extra helping of chocolate ice cream they were given. By the time they left the hall, the sun had set and stars had begun to appear in the dark sky.

"That earl with the black shoes has a room just along the corridor from me," said Lulu. "Let's go and hide nearby so we can see what he gets up to after dinner."

"Great idea!" said Emily. "I want to know what he's doing. I don't trust him one little bit."

They climbed the first set of stairs and walked down the corridor. As they went round a corner, Jaminta caught sight of someone slipping into the shadows behind them.

She flicked her fan open and whispered behind it, "There's someone spying on us! Over there!"

The girls froze.

"What should we do? Should we run away?" muttered Clarabel behind her fan.

"No! Let's pretend we haven't seen them," said Lulu. "Just keep walking."

The princesses climbed up the next staircase. As they reached the top, a shadowy figure moved through the darkness behind them for a second time.

Jaminta felt a tingle run down her spine. She recognised that ninja move.

Ally had taught it to them many months ago, when they were together at Mistberg Castle. She bit her lip. There was definitely someone sneaking after them, someone who didn't want to be seen.

Glancing back nervously, the princesses scurried down the corridor. Halfway along, Jaminta ducked behind a large dragon statue, making sure she was well hidden by its wooden body. She looked at the others and put a finger to her lips. They nodded quickly and carried on walking.

Jaminta crouched down, waiting, her heart thumping.

The shadow flitted closer. It paused for a moment by an open doorway. Then it moved a little nearer.

Jaminta held her breath as she watched the shadow edging towards her. What if the ninja had already seen her? For a

moment she wished she hadn't hidden here without her friends. But it was too late now. Feeling shaky inside, she jumped out from behind the dragon statue.

"Stop right now!" she called out, trying to sound brave.

The shadow shrieked and almost fell against the statue.

Jaminta grabbed the shadow's arm to hold it steady.

"Oh, thank you!" said a muffled voice.

Jaminta felt a shock run through her. "Ally? Is that you?" she asked.

The shadow unwound a dark scarf from around her chin. "Yes, it's me!" Ally said, more clearly this time. "Goodness, Jaminta! You made me jump!"

"But, Ally?" Jaminta stared at her. "I don't understand. What's going on? Why are you following us around in the dark?"

Chapter Seven

The Ten-Year Secret

The other princesses raced up to them.

"Ally! What are you doing?" said Emily, astonished. "You told me you were fixing the bow on my ball gown this evening!"

"You were sneaking after us!" said Lulu, her lion-like eyes flashing.

"No! Not at all!" exclaimed Ally, taking off a black woollen hat and letting her ponytail swing free. "I'm sorry, Your Majesties. I can see why you thought I was following you, but that's not what I

was doing at all."

"But you're wearing dark clothes for camouflage," Jaminta pointed out. "And using the ninja moves that you taught us."

"Yes," laughed Ally. "Although I'm obviously not as good as I used to be, because you spotted me easily. You girls are better at the moves than I am." She sighed a little.

The princesses stared at her, a million questions flying through their heads.

"Ally?" said Emily, at last. "Is there something secret going on?"

Ally looked serious. "We'd better go somewhere more private, where we can talk."

"My room's the closest," said Jaminta.

So they hurried into Jaminta's room. Emily, Clarabel and Lulu settled down on the plump green sofa, while Jaminta lay across the four-poster bed. They looked expectantly at Ally.

"So why *were* you being a ninja?" asked Jaminta.

"All right, I'll tell you," said Ally. "Ten years ago, when I was working as an undercover agent, I was given a very important case. I was asked to find the missing Onica Heart Crystals and catch the thief who stole them."

"Heart Crystals? Were they really famous?" asked Clarabel.

"The Onica Heart Crystals were the most precious jewels in the whole kingdom," explained Jaminta. "There were four of them, each one in the shape of a heart. They were clear, just like diamonds, but had a flickering flame right in the middle. Grandfather told me that he used to keep them in a glass case in the banquet hall. Then one morning

they were gone."

"They were beautiful jewels," Ally agreed. "And really powerful too. They were supposed to show a person's true nature and whether they were good or horrid."

"I've never heard of a jewel that could do that before!" said Emily.

"So what happened after they were stolen?" asked Lulu.

"I investigated the robbery for months and months. I followed the trail across the ocean to the Kingdom of Middingland." Ally's eyes flicked to Emily, the Middingland princess. "I was there to spy on someone suspicious. But I never managed to find the jewels and finally I was told to give up. I was working as a maid in Middingland Palace at the time and I liked it so much that I stayed there."

Emily's mouth dropped open. "Do you mean, you were an undercover agent when you became our maid? So being a maid was part of your disguise?"

"It was only a disguise at first." Ally smiled at her. "That was ten years ago. But I could never quite forget the Onica Heart Crystals. They were such special jewels."

A scuffling sound on the roof made them all jump.

Lulu dashed out on to the dark balcony and came back a few seconds later. "It's all right," she panted. "It's only an owl."

"But I still don't understand why you were sneaking down the corridor," said Clarabel.

"I always wondered whether the stolen Heart Crystals were actually still here in the Kingdom of Onica. Maybe the robber hid them somewhere nearby because he knew we suspected him," explained Ally. "So when I saw the man I spied on ten years ago, I couldn't help following him."

"You must be talking about someone from Middingland!" cried Emily.

"Who is it, Ally? You have to tell us!" said Lulu.

"I don't think I should," said Ally. "I don't want to get you into trouble."

Jaminta frowned for a moment, then her eyes widened. Ally had looked at someone very suspiciously that morning. Jaminta remembered the mysterious look she'd had in her eyes.

Ally got up. "Now I must get back to mending the bow on that ball gown. After that I'll bring you all some mugs of hot chocolate."

As Ally disappeared from the room, Emily turned to the others. "I can't believe Ally kept her secret about why she came to Middingland all this time!"

"I wonder if she's right and the jewels are hidden somewhere nearby," said Lulu excitedly.

"But if they're hidden here, wouldn't someone have discovered them by now?" said Clarabel.

"The jewels ARE hidden here! Don't you see!" Jaminta leapt up, her brown eyes shining. "Ten years ago, Ally went to Middingland to investigate the thief. Emily, you said that Earl Scrant lives in Middingland! And when we hid under that table, we heard him say he wants to dig up something from the mountainside. So he must be digging up the stolen Heart Crystals!"

Chapter Eight

The Magical River

Emily, Clarabel and Lulu looked at each other, their eyes widening.

"I hadn't thought of that!" said Emily. "I think you're right, Jaminta. Earl Scrant must have stolen the jewels and then buried them on the mountainside in a hurry because he knew he might be caught."

"But what shall we do about it?" said Clarabel. "Would your grandfather really believe all this, Jaminta?"

Jaminta shook her head. "We haven't got any real proof. We can only tell him what we heard while we were hidden under a table."

"Then we have to make sure we're there when Earl Scrant digs up the Heart Crystals," said Lulu. "If he's caught carrying them, everyone will know he was the thief."

"We can use our ninja moves to follow him," said Emily.

"He won't go up the mountain in the dark, so we can start tomorrow morning, straight after we've taken my rock crystal to the river," added Jaminta.

Lulu and Emily exchanged glances.

"I think we should just concentrate on following Earl Scrant and forget about your crystal," said Lulu.

Emily nodded. "We don't want to miss our chance to find out where the earl will be digging."

"But I have to take the crystal to the river at sunrise. The Master Gem Maker told me to!" cried Jaminta.

Lulu tapped her foot impatiently on the floor. "But this mystery with the earl and the Heart Crystals is *way* more exciting! Anyway, we might get to see Lucky the panda cub again while we're up the mountain!"

"I hope we do!" cried Emily. "He's so adorable! Maybe this time we could pick him some bamboo to eat."

"You shouldn't get too close to Lucky," said Jaminta. "He doesn't know you very well so he might get scared."

"Oh, don't worry!" said Lulu. "We're Rescue Princesses! I think we know how to take care of animals by now."

Jaminta frowned. She wasn't sure she wanted the other girls getting too close to her cub. After all, she was the one who'd been watching him ever since he was a new born panda. She was the one who knew him best of all.

"I know!" said Clarabel. "Maybe Jaminta and I could go to the river at sunrise, while you two keep an eye on Earl Scrant and find out what he's up to."

"That's a good idea!" said Emily. "That way you can still finish off making your new crystal, Jaminta."

Jaminta smiled weakly. She couldn't help wishing she could be at the river *and* up the mountain with her panda cub all at once. "All right, then," she said. "And after we've finished making the jewel, we'll come to find you as quickly as we can."

Jaminta watched her grandfather's fireworks from her balcony that night.

Huge bursts of red and gold blossomed up into the dark sky and twinkled as they fell. After they had ended, she climbed into bed and shut her eyes.

Her mind was buzzing with thoughts. Would the river really change the rock crystal? And would Earl Scrant discover where he'd buried the Heart Crystals all those years ago? She turned over and rubbed her eyes, and fell asleep thinking about Lucky.

💜

She woke the other princesses early the next morning while it was still dark outside. They sneaked downstairs together, only to find Earl Scrant standing in the hallway as if he was waiting for someone. He raised his eyebrows when he saw them and marched away, frowning.

"Do you think he knows that we've worked out he stole the Heart Crystals?"

whispered Clarabel.

"I don't know," said Emily. "But he won't see us following him if we use our best ninja moves."

"We'd better go down to the river now, Clarabel. It's nearly sunrise," said Jaminta awkwardly, wishing they were all going together.

"Good luck with your rock crystal," said Emily.

"Thanks." Jaminta bit her lip. "And please be careful about getting close to Lucky. He gets scared quite easily."

"Don't worry!" said Lulu firmly. "We know what to do. Come on, Emily!"

The princesses walked out of the palace door and hurried across the garden. Lulu and Emily stopped halfway along the path and waved goodbye to the others. Then they hid behind a large statue of a soldier.

Jaminta and Clarabel raced on, out of the back gate and down the hill, their hair flying out behind them. The sun hadn't risen yet, but the sky was turning from grey to pale yellow. The river lay at the bottom of the valley like a long glittering ribbon.

"I can see why it's called the Silver River," said Clarabel. "It's so beautiful."

Slowing down, they slipped off their shoes and walked right to the edge of the riverbank, where ducks dabbled in the clear water. Shoals of tiny blue fish darted to and fro under the surface. The girls bent over to look at them, making two princess reflections in the water.

"I wish we were all together," sighed Jaminta. "Do you think Lulu still believes that my crystal is dangerous because of the rock fall yesterday?"

"Maybe, but I'm sure she'll change her

mind when she sees its new shape," said Clarabel. "It's really exciting. I've never seen a jewel changed by magic before."

"I really hope it works!" Jaminta waded into the shallows, holding the lump of crystal in one hand. Carefully, she lowered the gem into the water until it lay still on the sandy riverbed. Then she climbed back out and sat on the bank.

"How long will it take?" said Clarabel.

Jaminta stared into the swirling river. "I don't know. The Master Gem Maker didn't say."

But as they watched, the crystal seemed to grow. Its sides quivered and moved, almost as if it was alive. Then finally, it settled into a new shape. Not just a lump of whitish rock any more. Now it was the most beautiful thing they had ever seen, lying sparkling beneath the water.

Chapter Nine

The Star Crystal

The two princesses stared at the jewel.

"It's a star!" cried Jaminta.

"Wow, that's amazing!" said Clarabel.

The gem glowed, filling the water with light. Then the brightness faded.

Jaminta waded back in and lifted out the Star Crystal just as the sun rose over the tops of the mountains. She held it up to the sun's first rays and caught her breath. The jewel was now as clear and sparkling as a diamond, and right in the centre there was a beautiful flickering fire.

"Is there supposed to be a flame inside it?" said Clarabel, looking alarmed.

"Yes! That's exactly how the Heart Crystals look in all the old pictures." Jaminta turned the Star Crystal over in her hand. Grandfather was going to be so happy with his present. "I wonder if it still makes a singing sound, like it did before," she added, thoughtfully.

"You're not taking it up the mountain, are you?" gasped Clarabel. "What if something bad happens?"

"It won't," Jaminta said calmly. "I believe in this jewel. The power inside it is good."

Clarabel looked doubtfully at the Star Crystal, which shone in the growing sunshine.

Just then a great black and white shape

came out of the bamboo forest on the other side of the river. The mother panda lumbered down the slope and stopped for a moment, pointing her nose towards the two princesses. Then she took a few more strides down to the water and bent her head to drink.

"I've never seen her come right down to the river before," said Jaminta.

"Where's Lucky?" said Clarabel, peering hopefully at the forest.

The panda cub sprang out of the trees and frolicked across the grass towards his mother. He drank from the river for a second, then sat back on his bottom and scratched his furry white tummy with one paw. A bumblebee flew past his nose and he half stood up to swipe at it, but fell over backwards instead. His little legs waved wildly in the air.

Jaminta and Clarabel giggled.

"I wish we could stay and watch him all day. He's so cute," sighed Clarabel.

Jaminta put her new Star Crystal into her pocket. "I suppose we should find the others though," she began, but she broke off when her emerald ring lit up brightly. Clarabel's sapphire ring started to glow as well and a faint voice came through.

"Jaminta? Clarabel? It's Emily! Can you hear me?" Emily's voice sounded worried.

"We can hear you," said Jaminta. "What is it?"

"The earl and his servant are heading your way. Try to follow them," said Emily. "We had to stay away from them because they spotted us and—" Emily's voice crackled and broke off.

Jaminta pressed the emerald on her ring, but the light had vanished.

"Look, Jaminta! Here's the earl," hissed Clarabel.

Two figures came striding out of the back gate and down the hill towards them. The girls pretended to be looking for fish in the river. The man in front was tall and thin, with a crooked mouth and a red cloak that swirled behind him. It was definitely Earl Scrant.

"The servant's got a shovel," muttered Clarabel. "They must be planning to dig for the Heart Crystals right now."

Jaminta tried to glance at them quickly so that they didn't see her looking. She saw the earl's swirling red cloak out of the corner of her eye and it reminded her of something. She'd seen a glimpse of that red cloak before, by the bridge yesterday after they'd visited the pandas.

Earl Scrant climbed on to the curved bridge and stopped to glare at the two princesses.

"Hey, look Clarabel!" Jaminta pointed

at the water and spoke loudly, her heart thumping. "I just saw some fish."

Both girls leaned over the water, pretending to look.

"Come on, Drudger! Get a move on!" snapped the earl.

The other man followed the earl across the bridge, carrying the shovel balanced over one shoulder. As they reached the other side, the mother panda walked back into the forest, leaving the cub still playing on the riverbank.

Jaminta and Clarabel tiptoed forward. They crept across the bridge, taking care not to make a sound. The two men stopped next to the trees and unfolded a large map.

The princesses edged closer, listening.

"We'll turn right after the rope bridge," said the earl. "Then I'll look for more landmarks."

Jaminta crept a little nearer, but her shoe caught on a twig and it broke beneath her foot with an enormous crack.

The earl swung round, his eyes bulging. "You dratted princesses! How dare you follow me?"

The other man scowled. "That's four of them. If you count the ones we saw in the garden, hiding behind that statue."

The earl ground his teeth. "Keep away from me or I'll make you regret it!"

"We're just going." Jaminta turned pale. "We won't disturb you." She and Clarabel started backing away, their hearts thumping.

But the earl took no notice. He had caught sight of the panda cub scampering by the river. He strode over to Lucky and snatched up the little cub with one gloved hand.

"I know what will stop your meddling," he snapped. "See this pathetic creature that you were cooing over when you crossed the bridge yesterday? Well, if you follow me or if you tell anyone at the palace where I've gone, then you'll never ever see him again!"

Jaminta's heart turned cold. He was threatening poor Lucky!

The earl gave a horrible twisted smile. "Do you understand? If you tell or if you follow me, something bad will happen to this silly animal." He stowed the cub under one arm. "And there are some very steep drops on the mountainside, if you know what I mean." Chuckling to himself, the earl marched away into the bamboo forest, with his servant behind him.

Clarabel turned to Jaminta, tears in her eyes. "What shall we do? He's taken

 329

Lucky and it's all our fault."

Lulu and Emily came sprinting across the wooden bridge.

"What happened?" panted Lulu. "We saw Earl Scrant talking to you. What did he say?"

Jaminta brushed tears from her eyes. "He picked up Lucky and took him away. He said if we followed him, we'd never see Lucky again."

"Oh no!" Emily put her hand over her mouth.

"But we can't leave Lucky with him. He's a dangerous man," cried Clarabel.

Lulu frowned furiously. "I brought some rope in this backpack. Maybe we can capture the earl and tie him up."

"No, he's too big. We'd never manage it. We'll have to think of something else." Jaminta gazed up at the mountain, a feeling of calm settling over her. Suddenly she knew exactly what she had to do. "I know how we can get Lucky back. All we have to do is offer Earl Scrant something he really wants as a swap."

"What do you mean?" said Emily.

Jaminta drew her hand from her pocket and showed them the beautiful star-shaped jewel. "We give him this. We give him the Star Crystal."

"But, Jaminta!" cried Clarabel. "It's your new jewel. You wanted to give it to your grandfather for his birthday."

Jaminta sighed. "I know. But keeping Lucky safe is more important than anything else in the world!"

"Did your lump of crystal really change into that?" Emily's eyes widened.

Jaminta nodded. "And when the earl sees it, I know he'll want it."

"But are you sure it's safe to take your jewel up there?" asked Lulu. "You know what happened last time."

"I'm totally sure," said Jaminta firmly.

"Quickly! Or we'll never find Lucky," urged Clarabel.

The four princesses flung themselves

into the forest. Jaminta took the lead, stopping to listen now and then, checking the direction of the men crashing through the bamboo trees up ahead. She leapt over a pile of stones and ran on. It was hard trying to be fast and quiet at the same time, but they had to make sure the earl didn't hear them until the very last second.

They stopped at the edge of the rocky ravine.

"This is where we crossed the valley yesterday," said Lulu. "But where's the rope bridge?"

Jaminta pointed down into the ravine, her cheeks flushing angrily. The rope bridge dangled down against the rocky cliff. "It's broken. Earl Scrant must have crossed over and then cut through the rope on the other side."

"What are we going to do?" said

Clarabel. "We can't climb all the way down there. It's way too steep."

Jaminta bit her lip. "We have to try something. We have to get to Lucky."

Lulu took off her backpack, reached inside it and pulled out a long coil of rope. "I'll climb over. Then I can tie one end of this rope to a tree and throw the other end across to you."

The princesses looked across the ravine. The biggest tree on the other side had sturdy branches, strong enough to swing from.

"Will you be able to do it?" Emily looked down at the steep cliff.

Lulu grinned. "Of course! I love climbing!"

She clambered carefully down the rock face, finding handholds and footholds in the rough cliff. Little by little, she lowered herself down.

"You're doing great!" Jaminta called softly as Lulu reached the bottom and began climbing up the other side.

At the top, Lulu tied the rope firmly to a tree and threw the other end across to them.

Jaminta caught it. "Who wants to go first?"

Clarabel's face turned pale. "I can't! It's too far."

"Don't worry. We'll help you." Jaminta put the rope into her hand. "Ready?"

Jaminta and Emily stood behind Clarabel. With a huge push, they swung her across the ravine to Lulu, who caught her safely on the other side. Clarabel hugged Lulu in relief and waved to the others.

Emily swung across next. Then Jaminta stood alone on the edge of the cliff. She took the rope, trying not to look down.

There was no one left to push her. She would have to jump hard enough to swing herself all the way across. She lifted her chin. Lucky was probably really scared by now. She would do it for him.

She jumped. The ravine opened out below her, a steep drop filled with jagged rocks. She swung closer to the other side and just as she wondered if she would make it, three pairs of arms grabbed her.

"Wow!" she gasped, her feet thudding on the ground. "That was pretty scary."

"Right, let's carry on," said Lulu. "We don't want to lose track of the earl."

They hurried on, slipping in and out of the trees, and at last they heard the men moving up ahead. The earl sounded even grumpier than before.

"Hurry up, Drudger!" he snapped. "I want to dig up my jewels and then escape from Onica as fast as possible. But *you* are

slowing me down!"

"The shovel is heavy, Your Grace," came the panted reply.

"Shovel! Just be thankful you're not carrying this wretched squirming animal," said the earl. "If it wriggles again I'll drop it off the mountain. I'd drop it right now if I could be sure that those frilly princesses aren't following us. But they're tricky! They may have found another way around that ravine."

"But, My Lord? Do you know the right way back to the palace now that you've cut the rope bridge?"

There was a pause.

"I brought you here to dig, Drudger, not to think. I can work out the way back myself." The earl coughed uneasily. "This is the right place. I'm sure I buried my lovely Heart Crystals here. Start digging at once!"

The princesses crept forward and peered through the bamboo trees into the clearing. The earl still held Lucky carelessly under one arm. The little cub twisted anxiously and let out a tiny whimper. Jaminta longed to hug him and make him feel better.

"I wish we could tie up that nasty earl," hissed Lulu.

"Isn't this where we came before? When we first saw Lucky and that rock fall happened?" whispered Clarabel.

Jaminta glanced around the clearing and nodded. The skin on the back of her neck tingled. Something important was about to happen here. Somehow she just knew it was.

"Do you really think you should take the crystal in there?" said Emily.

Jaminta drew the Star Crystal from her pocket. Inside its diamond-clear shape, a flame burned brightly. "This is the only thing I've got that the earl will take in exchange for Lucky." She took a deep breath. "Ready, everyone?"

The others nodded. Together they stepped out of their hiding place into full view.

"You again!" yelled the earl. "This time you will be sorry!"

But Jaminta interrupted him. "Stop! We've come to ask for the panda cub in exchange for this crystal." She held the Star Crystal out for him to see.

The earl's eyebrows rose. "What? Where did you get that from?"

"Never mind where we got it!" said Jaminta, her voice trembling. "It's a Star Crystal and you can have it if you hand over the cub right now."

The earl strode towards her and snatched the Star Crystal out of her hand, dropping Lucky on the ground without a second thought.

Jaminta ran to Lucky, gathering the little cub into her arms and feeling his soft black and white fur against her cheek. "Lucky!" she whispered. "I'm so glad you're safe!"

Lucky mewed happily and snuffled into her ear.

The earl's face broke into a twisted smile of delight as he gazed at the sparkling Star Crystal. "This will truly make me rich!" He turned to his servant. "Now, Drudger! Tie up these nosy princesses!"

But the other man wasn't listening. He dropped his shovel and looked around with wide eyes. A sound began to rise above the bamboo trees, clear and sweet. The Star Crystal had started to sing.

Chapter Eleven

Sister Jewels

Jaminta backed away, holding Lucky tightly in her arms. The other princesses edged backwards too.

"What's going on?" moaned the earl.

The song became higher and more haunting, weaving around them like the wind. The earl dropped the Star Crystal and put his hands over his ears. The rocky outcrop behind the men began to shudder. The earth trembled. An enormous splinter of stone broke off and shattered on the ground below.

"The mountain's falling down!" cried the earl.

The two men ran away, stumbling over rocks and crashing through trees as they fled back down Cloud Mountain.

The princesses stood their ground. Jaminta held on to Lucky even tighter, while he buried his head in her shoulder.

The Star Crystal sang a final piercing note, which made the earth rumble and opened up a gaping hole in the ground. Then the song faded away to nothing and the mountainside stopped shaking. One last swirl of dust rose from the fallen stones and floated away.

Jaminta breathed deeply in the sudden silence. She looked around, stroking Lucky's soft fur. She was so glad that he was safe and no one had been hurt.

"That was weird," said Emily. "I felt like

the Star Crystal wanted something. Like it was talking."

Clarabel nodded. "I thought that too."

Lulu darted forward to look inside the hollow that had opened in the ground. "Come and see this! There's something in here." She climbed down into the hole and picked up a small brown sack lying at the bottom.

The girls gathered round as Lulu undid the string at the top and turned the sack upside down. Four beautiful heart-shaped crystals tumbled out on to the grass. Each one was sparkling and transparent, but with a tiny flame in the centre.

Clarabel picked one up. The Heart Crystal sparkled between her fingers.

"The Onica Heart Crystals!" gasped Jaminta. "Grandfather will be so happy that they've been found!"

"So will Ally!" said Emily. "I can't wait

to tell her!"

"You were right, your crystal wasn't a bad jewel at all," said Lulu. "We should have believed you, Jaminta."

Jaminta smiled back at them. "I knew it couldn't be bad. It must have been trying to find the Heart Crystals all along. It was singing to set them free." She gave Lucky a squeeze and patted his furry tummy.

Emily picked up the Star Crystal from where the earl had dropped it and laid it next to the Heart Crystals. The five gems glowed together for a second. "Look! They're like sister jewels."

Behind them came a loud rustling and the mother panda lumbered into the clearing. Lucky let out a soft mew and licked Jaminta's hand.

"There you go, little Lucky." Jaminta set him gently down on to the ground.

"He's safe now that the earl's run

away," said Emily.

Lucky gambolled over to his mother, who nuzzled him lovingly.

Jaminta smiled as she watched them amble away across the grass. Lucky turned to look at her one more time before he followed his mother into the forest.

Jaminta picked up the jewels and gave one Heart Crystal to each of her friends.

"Let's go back to the palace and show these jewels to my grandfather," she said. "It will be a perfect birthday present for him!"

Chapter Twelve

The Heart Crystals Come Home

The princesses hurried through the palace gate. It had taken them a long time to find a way back that avoided the rocky ravine with its broken rope bridge. A loud cheer rose as they walked into the garden. The girls looked at each other in surprise, but the crowd of people standing on the grass were all facing the other way.

"What's going on?" whispered Clarabel.

Jaminta tried to peer through the mass

of people, but she could only see arms and legs.

"Your grandfather's standing next to his birthday cake," called Lulu, who had climbed halfway up the soldier statue. "I think we're going to sing Happy Birthday to him next."

Jaminta's mum noticed the girls and frowned at the sight of their muddy dresses. "Princesses! Where have you been? Jaminta, you're absolutely covered in dirt and leaves. Go upstairs and change at once!"

"But, Mum! We've found something really amazing," said Jaminta, trying to show her the Heart Crystal. "And I don't want to miss grandfather's party."

"Jaminta! You can't stand here with twigs in your hair!" said the Queen of Onica, sternly.

Jaminta swept a hand over her dark

hair and pulled out a clump of twigs. She pulled a face and turned towards the palace.

"Is that my lovely grand-daughter?" called Emperor Cho from the front. "Come up here, Jaminta!"

Jaminta brushed the leaves off her dress and made her way through the crowd until she stood next to her grandfather. "Happy birthday, Grandfather!" she said, hugging him. "I've got a special present to give you!"

Her grandfather's eyes twinkled. "Is it a surprise?"

Jaminta grinned. "I guess it is! You see, I tried to make a beautiful crystal to give to you and it finally worked." She dropped the Star Crystal into his wrinkled hand. "And then this star jewel helped me find these crystals as well." She dropped one of the Heart Crystals into his hand, too.

Emperor Cho stared at the magical crystals in silent amazement. Lulu, Emily and Clarabel came to the front and showed him the other three heart-shaped gems.

"Happy birthday, Grandfather!" said Jaminta softly.

"The stolen crystals!" said the emperor, gazing at the sparkling jewels. "How did you find them after all this time?"

"They were buried on the mountainside," explained Jaminta. "The thief hid them there, planning to dig them up later."

"But who was it that hid them?" The emperor looked all around, as if he was expecting the thief to jump out of the crowd.

"It was Earl Scrant, Your Majesty!" said Emily, with a curtsy. "We saw him trying to dig up the jewels today."

"Really? Earl Scrant?" echoed the emperor in astonishment.

The kings and queens muttered to each other and shook their heads.

"Look! There he is!" someone called, and the crowd turned to look at a tall, thin figure that was hurrying towards the palace gates with a suitcase.

"Guards! Arrest him!" called Emperor Cho.

Earl Scrant saw the guards chasing him and began to run. He dropped his suitcase, which sprang open and Jaminta's tiara fell out on to the drive. The crowd gasped. The earl was caught by the guards and taken away.

"Well, this *is* a day of big surprises!" said the emperor. "I'm so very proud of you, Jaminta. You discovered something that has been lost for ten years."

The queen sniffed. "I *suppose* you did

very well to find them, even though your dresses are rather dirty."

Jaminta chewed her lip. "But . . . I nearly gave all these jewels away to save a panda cub."

Her grandfather burst out laughing. "That's because you're a kind-hearted girl. Have I ever told you the true power of these Heart Crystals?"

Jaminta shook her head.

Emperor Cho gave her the heart-shaped jewel back. "Blow on the crystal very gently. You try it too, girls."

The princesses all blew gently on the Heart Crystals. As their breath touched the jewels, their transparent surfaces filled with beautiful colour. Jaminta's gem turned green, Emily's was red, Clarabel's was blue and Lulu's was bright yellow. A murmur of astonishment rippled around the crowd.

"They've turned the same colours as our rings," whispered Jaminta.

"These crystals show the true nature of a person's heart," said the emperor. "I suspect if Earl Scrant blew on one of these gems it would turn black, revealing him for the scoundrel he is. But each of you has a very good heart indeed."

The crowd clapped and cheered.

"And I want you to keep this star jewel, Jaminta," the emperor continued, "to remind you of this special day. Having these Heart Crystals back is enough of a birthday present for me."

"Thank you, Grandfather!" said Jaminta.

"Well done, princesses!" whispered Ally, who had come to see the celebrations. "Ten years after they vanished, the Heart Crystals are finally back where they belong."

Emperor Cho asked his guards to put the Heart Crystals away safely in a display cabinet in the banquet hall. Then they all sang Happy Birthday and ate several slices of cake. The twelve-tier birthday cake kept everyone happy, with its layers of chocolate fudge cake, cherry and sultana cake, ginger, lemon, toffee and many other flavours. Emily's little sister, Lottie, ate a slice from all twelve tiers and then had to sit very still on a garden chair to calm her aching tummy.

Jaminta linked arms with the others as they went to fetch glasses of lemonade. "I know we don't agree all the time, but I'll never forget all the things we've done together."

"Me neither," said Lulu.

"The adventures just get better and better," said Clarabel, with a happy sigh.

"Maybe one day we'll find more

princesses who'd like to join us," said
Emily, skirting round her sister, Lottie,
who was now turning cartwheels across
the garden.

"I'm sure lots of girls would love to
join," agreed Jaminta. "After all, who
could say no to a life full of jewels,
banquets and ninja training?"

Collect the series!